MARSTON— MASTER SPY

MALCOLM SAVILLE

Girls Gone By Publishers

COMPLETE AND UNABRIDGED

Published by Girls Gone By Publishers
The Vicarage, Church Street, Coleford, Radstock, Somerset, BA3 5NG
www.ggbp.co.uk

First published by William Heinemann Ltd 1978
First published by Girls Gone By Publishers 2022
Text © the Estate of Malcolm Saville
Introduction © Stephen Bigger 2022
Publishing History © Stephen Bigger 2022
Note on the Text © Sarah Woodall 2022
Design and Layout © Girls Gone By Publishers 2022

Cover design by Ken Websdale
Typeset in England by GGBP
Printed and bound by Short Run Press, Exeter

ISBN 978-1-84745-310-5

CONTENTS

INTRODUCTION

Before the GGBP editions, the Marston Baines series (1963–1978) was difficult to purchase: titles were rarely reprinted and were never in paperback. *Marston—Master Spy* was the rarest with only one printing. It is clear from his letters to Mary Cadogan (now held by the Malcolm Saville Society), which I have reproduced online (http://eprints.worc.ac.uk/799 and 1332), that Saville regarded the series as a significant legacy that needed to be available in paperback. This edition of the last story in the series fulfils that dream. His estimation draws on the Christian message of good overcoming evil, a conservative theology without nuance, with good and evil as polar opposites, extremes at war with each other. We have to choose between them.

The original publisher's blurb (reproduced on the back of this GGBP edition) declares this title to be the last of the series. Unlike the previous three stories, it is not called 'A Marston Baines Thriller'. It is also the only title in the series with a dedication—'To my wife'. The title page has a short Epigraph: 'The only thing necessary for the triumph of evil, is that good men should do nothing—Edmund Burke, 1795'. The mysterious visitor in the first chapter reveals that the fictional Marston has used this in his last thriller, also. Although a common quotation today, it raises problems. Burke was an over-cautious traditionalist Irish politician. The origin of this quotation in his writings has never been discovered, although he did say something vaguer in 1770—that when evil people get together, good people must combine against them—of which the wording used in the epigraph may be a paraphrase (*Oxford Dictionary of Quotations*, 1996, pp159–160). There is no mention of it in the 1960 Penguin *Dictionary of Quotations*. President Kennedy used this form of words in 1961, attributing it to Burke, and thanks to that it appeared in Penguin's 1968 edition (the source cited was a 1795 letter), but this was a dead end, and subsequent editions omitted the entry. That was Saville's source, the words 'good' and 'evil' ideally suiting his plot.

Mark O'Hanlon (2001, p124) dates the Savilles' Luxembourg holiday to May 1975. The story's Foreword refers to the Luxembourg castle of Vianden as 'ruins'. Since then it has been extensively restored. Saville calls the area 'Little Switzerland', a name which technically applies to the environs around the medieval town of Echternach on the German border, about 20 corkscrew kilometres from Vianden. He states that most other location details are fictional, as is the reported bribing of local police officers. His statement of aims is worth quoting: 'this adventure deals with the age-old conflict between good and evil. Virtually no day passes without the reporting of tyranny, violence, unrest, revolt, terrorism and the attempted overthrow of personal freedom'. The same is still true, and James Bond, one inspiration for Marston Baines, still resonates today. So what Saville says next is interesting and timely:

> It is also true that the Soviet Union, through the world-wide use of its secret agents (known as KGB) is working continually in all countries to alter opinion and policy in their own interests. This organization is probably the greatest and most successful spy system the world has ever known. The KGB's agents, unsuspected, are in many positions of influence both in Britain and America. They use bribes and blackmail to enslave new agents to work for them.

> We, on the other hand, seek 'to maintain freedom and justice

and to fight tyranny'. It is true that the USSR far outspent any other country on espionage. Also relevant is the Granada TV drama production *Philby, Burgess and Maclean*, starring Derek Jacobi, shown on 31 May 1977 when Saville's final Baines story was being written. Kim Philby was a master spy who had risen high in MI6 and the British Embassy in Washington DC, and without being suspected passed everything of significance to Moscow during and after the Second World War. Burgess and Maclean were unmasked in 1951 and fled to Moscow, but Philby spied until 1963 before also defecting to Moscow. This clearly is the background of Saville's comments on the KGB.

Saville was also a fan of John Le Carré. Le Carré, real name David Cornwell (1930–2020), worked for MI6, the 'foreign' secret service, until his retirement in 1964 after Philby had passed details of British agents to the KGB. His first thriller, *Call for the Dead* (1961), introduced George Smiley and 'the Circus' (named after its office in Cambridge Circus, London). The pen-name Le Carré humorously translates as 'The Square'. In *Tinker, Tailor, Soldier, Spy* (1974) everyone in 'the Circus' is suspected of being the top Russian agent, the 'mole' (double agent). The unidentified 'mole' in Le Carré's George Smiley stories is based on Philby.

Marston Baines mimics Le Carré as both master spy and thriller writer. (*Call for the Dead* also has a spy-master named Maston.) Le Carré's *The Spy Who Came in from the Cold* (1963) is obliquely referred to in *Marston—Master Spy* (p116). Saville openly declares Britain's enemy (and hence Marston's, too) to be the KGB. Marston also describes a certainly fictional KGB operative nicknamed 'The Great Bear' as having significance in our story. The 'Great Bear' is normally the USSR's nickname.

Luxembourg
Saville would have used the Michelin *Green Guide* for his visit. There

are several other travel guides also available today. The Duchy is about the size of Derbyshire, mountainous in the Ardennes (in the north) and with good farmland in the south around Luxembourg City, now a financial capital. Once rich from mining and steel, today the country gets its wealth from banking and finance. There are borders with Germany to the north-east, with Belgium to the north-west and with France to the south. The Ardennes region is an ideal hiking area, though rather hilly for bicycles. There is a railway, but towns like Vianden depend on bus services. Along the German border is the River Our (pronounced like 'oar'). The 'Our National Park' includes Vianden.

The Ardennes was the location of a Second World War liberation battle as the American army advanced; the Nazis planned to form a defensive line at Antwerp. Their defeat was inevitable, so the deaths and casualties on both sides were entirely avoidable and indefensible—30,000 were American, 52,000 German, 1000 British and 4000 locals. The Grand Duchess Charlotte (the head of state, Luxembourg being a constitutional monarchy like the UK) escaped to Canada and broadcast loyal messages into occupied Luxembourg. Forbidden to speak French, the local people refused to speak German, and so there was a revival of 'Luxembourgish'.

Saville describes the trunk road to Luxembourg City as the 'E40 from Brussels to Luxembourg' (p86). Today that road is numbered E411, and the upgraded E40 bypasses Brussels and continues to Liege and beyond. The E40 is now the longest European Route at 8000 km (5000 miles). My 1970s road map, bought for a French holiday, does mark the bendy Brussels–Luxembourg road as E40, but not yet as a dual carriageway.

To meet his contact in Luxembourg City, Simon has to cross a bridge over a ravine, at the bottom of which two rivers flow, the Alzette and the Pétrusse. The 'Pétrusse Ravine' has been developed as a public park, misspelled in the book as La Patrusse. He finds his contact in a record shop near the main railway station. He is to ask for a cassette of Marlene Dietrich singing 'Where have all the flowers gone?', a song written by Pete Seeger in 1955 with two additional verses later added by Joe Hickerson. It came to prominence when sung by Peter, Paul and Mary (1962) and was then sung by Dietrich in French at a UNICEF concert (*'Qui peut dire où vont les fleurs?'*); she also recorded it in German (*'Sag' mir, wo die Blumen sind'*) and English. She sang the English version on television at the Royal Variety Performance in 1963. Simon asks specifically for 'the English version'. There were many later covers which a casual purchaser might have asked for, so the Dietrich version was a safe choice, as the story indicates: 'Not likely that anyone else will ask him for that particular song' (p88). It is no surprise that a man of Saville's age and experience should remember Dietrich with affection. Today her versions are on YouTube.

Vianden is a small picturesque town on the German border. It had, Saville says, a rose-red ruined castle on a hill. Built between the 11th and 14th centuries, the castle's chapel, dedicated to St Anthony, was both castle chapel and town church (there was an early problem when the Trinitarians were allowed to use the chapel, annoying the Templars who thought they had the monopoly; a separate Templar Church, St Nicholas, was built in the town). A very ornate mezzanine was used by the castle family and the lower plain chapel by the townsfolk. If Saville was able to visit the chapel (it would have been ruined), he would have planned to describe the black magic happening at the bottom and the onlookers being on the mezzanine.

The castle was inherited by the Nassau family, the royal family, in the 17th century. Disaster came in 1820: the Grand Duke sold the castle to the highest bidder, a builder who wished to demolish it to sell the stone. After protests it was bought back but maintained only as a ruin. In 1977 the castle was gifted to the nation and restoration began. Much had been achieved by 1981, and work continued during the following decade; it now attracts a quarter of a million tourists each year. The artwork on the cover of *Marston—Master Spy* shows Vianden Castle as a ruin. We are told that the fictional house under suspicion, *Les Pins*, The House of the Pines, adjoins the castle and may have underground tunnels into it and into the chapel.

The Story

It is around Easter, when primroses are in flower. May Day is approaching. Rosina is now Simon's fiancée, and Charles Hand and Kate (née Boston) are married, so the List of Characters tells us (their marriage is a story not told in the series). Marston will be kidnapped, and black magic will be involved, says the blurb. The kidnap happens right at the beginning; wartime SOE and MI6 training should have prevented it. We learn about his cleaner (and her false teeth), and that Marston likes to type 2000 words a day, scrunching up unsatisfactory sheets, and that he dictates ideas into a cassette tape recorder. Maybe Saville is describing his own habits. Home computers were at prototype stage, Apple, Commodore and Tandy appearing in 1977. We have to remember that word processing, emails, URLs and hyperlinks were not embedded in desktops at this time and nothing was user-friendly. I visited IBM in Basingstoke in 1977, when mainframe computers that filled a room had less processing power than a mobile phone does today.

In the next chapter we meet Peter Pendent and his wife Elizabeth, Marston's publishers. Elizabeth is called 'secretary' but is clearly a fully involved partner. The approaching marriage of Simon and Rosina is discussed in the light of Peter and Elizabeth having worked successfully together. Peter is set to replace Marston on his retirement, and the publisher, Pendents, is an MI6 front. Paul Schengen has been signed up as an author as he is suspected of serious offences. At a publishing event for Schengen, Rosina is described as attractive to men and good looking. She is dressed up like a mannequin in traditional Luxembourg dress to impress the guests:

> She looked lovely in a crimson, short-sleeved dress worn over a white blouse with long sleeves. Tied around her waist was a white apron with a gaily coloured embroidered border. Her hair was covered by a pleated, white muslin bonnet. Her stockings were white and her shoes black. (pp52–53)

No doubt Saville had holiday photos to work from, and postcards can still be found online. Women were defined by their appearance, their clothes and their make-up.

Simon and Rosina are invited to Luxembourg, Simon poached to a better job, and the plot is set. Marston has not shown up, of course, so Charles and Simon drive through the night to Marston's home while the 'girls' sleep on the back seat. They head past Croydon and East Grinstead on the A22 towards Willingate on the South Downs, described as having a distant view of the sea. Simon comments:

> 'I don't like this, Charlieboy. Wish we hadn't brought the girls. Do you think they'll stay outside while we search the house?'
>
> 'No they won't' Rosina whispered behind them. 'You've still got a lot to learn about women, Simon. Open the front door and we'll search the place and get it over' (p62).

Women, not 'girls'. Simon has an old-fashioned view about protecting her which represses her ability to act. She also says that Peter Pendent 'obviously doesn't believe I'm capable of looking after myself'. Simon calls her bitchy ('Don't be bitchy, darling', p86), to which, despite it making her feel rebellious, she feels she has to plead guilty ('Sorry, darling. I was bitchy again. Forgive me' p88). Jake (Simon's superior in Luxembourg) is unhappy about involving Rosina, though he recognises it might encourage Simon's acceptance—he places responsibility for her safety firmly on Simon's shoulders. Elizabeth Poynter, in *You Girls Stay Here* (2018, p48), finds that the male protectiveness in this series is usually counterbalanced by female initiative and protest.

Marston has left a clue on his tape recorder, a description of an electronics engineer named Jan Schmidt who has visited him while attending a conference in Eastbourne. The scene moves to green and leafy Uccle, a historic and well-to-do suburb on the southern edge of Brussels, home and final resting place of Hergé, creator of the Tintin books. Marston is brought to Jan Schmidt's home among the trees in this desirable area. Competent and efficient Mrs Schmidt is introduced as 'a pretty, dark woman who smiled a welcome' (p73), another male-gaze stereotype. I leave the story here to avoid spoilers.

The Problem of Good and Evil
Reference is made (p100) to the theme of Satanism and black magic that appeared in the earlier story *Dark Danger*, where blackmail and drugs draw people into the Black Mass, influenced by Denis Wheatley's *The Satanist* (1960). The goat's head effigy, asymmetrical and disharmonious decor, and inverted Christian imagery are all repeated here. Saville may have been influenced by press accounts of black magic using human remains such as in old Clophill church near Bedford in the 1960s. For Saville this is a final opportunity to engage in pro-Christian sentiments. The Lord's Prayer and a crucifix have power over Satanism. The Black Mass is described as blasphemy. The baying crowd reminds Simon of the Crucifixion.

> [Simon] remembered that Marston, during a long walk on the Sussex Downs above his cottage, had once taught him the fundamental truths of the war in which they were engaged.

He had stressed that there is always a war between good and evil, between freedom and slavery, between compassion and cruelty … He had warned him also that the enemies of freedom are to be found amongst those carefully selected and trained men and women who set out to break down a nation's morale and destroy a people's will to resist. (p108)

Simon thinks Marston a brave and compassionate man. Saville had lived through the era of Hitler, Stalin and Mao, where evil was tangible and heads of state were mass murderers. The philosopher Hannah Arendt, commenting on the Eichmann 1961 trial, described it as 'the banality of evil', evil normalised as daily work in the office. The trial concluded that obeying orders was not a valid defence, especially when this colluded with unethical policies.

Saville's stories embed a black-and-white vision of good and evil. Characters are either one or the other: the good are morally obliged to fight evil. This lies at the heart of thriller fiction, and is not much different from the less moralistic Fleming stories. Saville depicts the evil opposition as totally evil and beyond redemption. We know what they are doing, step by step, and readers hope that the good guys will get there in time. There are no nuances. In *Marston— Master Spy* Saville's identification of 'good' with Christianity explains why he thought the series so important. God is at war with Satan. Each side has its high priests and its recruitment strategies. Evil operates through violence, murder, blackmail, secrecy, slavery and sabotage; good operates through law, morality and good faith, with good people standing up against evil and working to overcome it. However, in reality people are complex and are capable of making selfless or selfish choices, of kindness or venom, of caring or hating. There is more evil in everyday life than in a Satanic Mass: in seeking to defraud vulnerable victims, in polluting the environment and not safeguarding the public, in the rich avoiding tax which supports the needy, and in corrupt public servants. It would have been good to see more of such nuances.

Saville has distanced himself from Fleming/Bond, having no sexual impropriety and not killing gratuitously, even though Marston is 'licensed to kill' in self defence. Marrying off his male and female main characters is not demanded by his plots and complicates an action thriller with a romance, which particularly impacts on our story. Readers will take different views on this, and I would not wish to impose my own. In comparison with John Le Carré, Saville's British Secret Service supports Queen and country, patriotism and moral certitude. The Christian God is on *our* side, Satan is on theirs. Le Carré the real spy knew that the situation was far more murky and self-serving, regarding life as cheap. British policy had unknown aims and could result in unintended deaths, as well as intended ones. Double agents were passing information (secrets) to both sides, and neither side inhabited the moral high ground. Espionage was a game played on behalf of the political elite whose purposes are not always clear. In a sense George Smiley was Le Carré (both lived in Cornwall, and both were master spies); similarly Marston Baines was Saville (who was only a spy in imagination), and Marston was also Le Carré (both were spies and thriller writers covering the 1950s and 1960s, and both were to be retired when their identities became known to the KGB). All this adds interest to our readings of *Marston—Master Spy*, which (unlike Fleming and Le Carré) dangerously used young adults as agents on the ground.

Locally, this book was reviewed enthusiastically. 'Lots of excitement and suspense. Also a romantic theme supplied by Simon Baines (Marston's nephew) and his fiancée Rosina' (*Evening Argus*, 18 May 1978, quoted in O'Hanlon (2001, p124)).

I end with a purple passage:

The wind moaned in the tree-tops of the forest and

occasionally a full moon broke through the scudding clouds and touched the turrets and battlements of the chateau with a silver finger. An owl cried as the forces of evil gathered in the cellars below and the cavalcade of rescuers came slowly up the hill. (p178)

Saville still hauntingly evokes the 'spirit of place'.

Stephen Bigger

References

Arendt, Hannah. *Eichmann in Jerusalem: a Report on the Banality of Evil*, Viking Press, 1963

Jeffery, Keith. *MI6: The History of the Secret Intelligence Service 1909–1949*, Bloomsbury, 2010

Le Carré, John. *The Spy Who Came in from the Cold*, Penguin, 1963

Le Carré, John. *Tinker, Tailor, Soldier, Spy*, Penguin, 1974

O'Hanlon, Mark. *Beyond the Lone Pine: A Biography of Malcolm Saville*, O'Hanlon, 2001

Poynter, Elizabeth. *You Girls Stay Here: Gender Roles in Popular British Children's Adventure Fiction, 1930–70,* Cambridge Scholars Publishing, 2018

Wheatley, Denis. *The Satanist*, Hutchinson, 1960

PUBLISHING HISTORY

The first and only edition of *Marston—Master Spy* was published by William Heinemann in May 1978, ISBN 434 96207 4, with dark grey boards and gilt lettering. It had 145 pages of story; there were 160 pages in total including title, dedication, preliminary pages and advertisements. Its pictorial dustwrapper (reproduced on the cover of this GGBP edition), featuring Simon and Rosina with Vianden castle behind, does not credit the artist. Its initial price was £3.50.

Stephen Bigger

MARSTON BAINES BIBLIOGRAPHY

1. *Three Towers in Tuscany*
2. *The Purple Valley*
3. *Dark Danger*
4. *White Fire*
5. *Power of Three*
6. *The Dagger & The Flame*
7. *Marston—Master Spy*

FURTHER INFORMATION

The Malcolm Saville Society, formed in 1994, publishes four magazines a year, has a lending library, and also organises Saville events. Please contact the Membership Registrar at Orchard House, 66 Derby Road, Draycott, Derbyshire DE72 3NJ, or email mystery@witchend.com

Social media:
www.witchend.com
www.facebook.com/MalcolmSaville
@MSavilleSociety

The Malcolm Saville Centenary website, created by the late John Allsup and now maintained by Martin and Belinda Collins, contains a wealth of material on Malcolm Saville and his books, with links to other useful sites: www.malcolmsaville.co.uk

Mark O'Hanlon has written *Beyond the Lone Pine: a Biography of Malcolm Saville* and *The Complete Lone Pine*. Details of these may be found at www.witchend.com

NOTE ON THE TEXT

This GGBP edition of *Marston—Master Spy* uses the text of the first edition. We have neither edited nor updated it, but we have corrected a few obvious typographical errors where we could be certain of what the author intended. We hope we have not introduced any further errors.

This book generally follows the '-ize' spelling style, so we have amended four isolated occurrences of '-ise' spellings to conform to this (emphasised, apologise, apologised and moralising). We have corrected one misspelling: 'reconnoitered'. We have standardised on 'judgement' rather than 'judgment': they appeared once each, but 'judgement' is much more usual in non-legal British English contexts.

We have added the missing circumflex accent on three instances of 'chateau' to match the majority usage. We have not altered the accent on the hotel name, 'La Fôret': it is consistent throughout the book and may be deliberate, rather than a mistake for 'La Forêt'. For consistency, however, we have amended one instance of 'Le Fôret' (p97) to 'La'. The other hotel name appears once as 'La Patrusse' (as Stephen Bigger notes on p8), but it is also given once as 'La Petrusse', and, since the author tells us that it is named after the real place (p95), we have chosen to standardise on the latter version, which is closer to the place name.

There are a few ungrammatical sentences, for example this on page 122: 'Of more importance is the fact that a girl called Maria, who was introduced to me by Schengen as his secretary, and has given Rosina the impression that she is terrified, and even a hint that we shall be unwise if we go back to the house.' It is tempting to remove the 'and' after the second comma, but the author may have intended something different, and we cannot consult him, so we have left it as it was. Similarly, we have not attempted to correct 'The man smiled, walked across to lock the shop door and pull down the blind.' (p89) or 'I can guess that as you served part of your apprenticeship with Marston that you share his views' (p92).

'At the meeting of many of his members in Brussels which I attended I was to visit any of the branches' (p117) is not ungrammatical, but it makes no sense—perhaps the author meant to write 'I was invited to visit', but it is not our policy to guess where we cannot be sure, so we have left it alone.

Punctuation and capitalisation

We have not attempted to correct Malcolm Saville's idiosyncratic use of commas, which is a feature of his style. We have, however, changed commas to full stops on page 41 before 'Peter?' and on page 72 before 'Marston remembered', and full stops to commas on page 153 in 'when I wished him good morning and said what a lovely day it was going to be. I could see', and near the bottom of page 131, after 'By the way, Simon'. We have also added a full stop after 'OK' on page 172. We are certain that these were typographical errors.

There are several sentences that end in question marks although they are technically not questions; this again is a feature of the author's style, and we have not altered them (for example, 'he remembered Marston and wondered what had happened to him?' on page 174). However, we have changed a full stop to a question mark on page 68, at the end of 'I have no doubt of your sincerity but what is all this to do with me, and why go to the trouble of abducting me'.

The usual style of quotation marks in the book is single, with double for quotes within quotes. We have amended a few places where single quotes were used within quotes, to conform to this style. We have not altered the double quotes used in the displayed passage on page 65, as the difference of style here appears to be intentional.

We have added an apostrophe in 'but its up to you' (p84), supplied the missing opening quotes at the start of the second full paragraph on page 90 and of the first full paragraph on page 144, and deleted an unnecessary second opening quotation mark in the middle of a speech (before 'Get on to London, Jake', p156).

Where we could identify a majority usage we have standardised the use of hyphens, so we have amended one 'man-servant' to 'manservant', one 'this set-up' to 'this set up' and one 'sitting room' to 'sitting-room', but we have left unchanged 'girl-friend'/'girl friend', 'cooperate'/'co-operate', 'cooperating'/'co-operating', 'counter-espionage'/'counter espionage' and 'air-conditioner'/'air conditioner'.

We have capitalised one instance of 'latin' and two of 'western' (pp92 and 130), which is generally capitalised in this book if the context is politics or culture. We have standardised on capitals for 'Satanism' and 'Satanist': the original usage varied. However, 'black mass' is in lower case consistently in the original book, so we have left it unchanged (although it is capitalised elsewhere in the Marston Baines series, for example in *Dark Danger*). The title of the song sung by Marlene Dietrich is capitalised in various different ways; there is no consistent pattern, so we have left these all as they were.

Following GGBP's usual policy, we have used an unspaced em-dash through the text in place of the spaced en-dashes in the original, and we have standardised the spacing of ellipses.

'St. Pancras' appears with a full stop and 'St Albans' without; we have left these unchanged.

Sarah Woodall

MALCOLM SAVILLE

Marston—Master Spy

The only thing necessary for the triumph of evil,
is that good men should do nothing.

Edmund Burke 1795

To my wife

CONTENTS

Foreword

It is important for the reader to realize that the events described in this story—and the characters—are imaginary. The actual background is real. Vianden exists and is the pride of that district of the Duchy of Luxembourg known as 'Little Switzerland'. If you are ever lucky enough to explore it you will see the ruins of a mighty castle crowning the hill above the town, but you will not find the house I have called Les Pins nor the Pop Shop in Luxembourg. And there is no such publisher as Peter Pendent in London.

It is hinted in this story that the local police in Luxembourg may have been influenced to cover up a crime. This suggestion is entirely without foundation.

Like the other six stories about Marston Baines and his young friends, this adventure deals with the age-old conflict between good and evil. Virtually no day passes without the reporting of tyranny, violence, unrest, revolt, terrorism and the attempted overthrow of personal freedom.

It is also true that the Soviet Union, through the worldwide use of its secret agents (known as the KGB) is working continually in all countries to alter opinion and policy in their own interests. This organization is probably the greatest and most successful spy system the world has ever known. The KGB's agents, unsuspected, are in many positions of influence both in Britain and America. They use bribes and blackmail to enslave new agents to work for them. People like Paul Schengen.

On the other side, engaged in a silent battle against heavy odds, are men and women pledged to maintain freedom and justice and to fight tyranny. Such people as Peter Pendent and young Simon Baines. And, of course, men growing old in the Service. Men like Marston Baines.

M.S.

Chelsea Cottage
Winchelsea
East Sussex

Characters

Marston Baines	Thriller writer and one-time British special agent and now ready for retirement
Simon Baines	Marston's nephew now training as special agent. Works for Peter Pendent
Peter Pendent	Marston's publisher and special agent who has taken over Marston's responsibilities
Jan Schmidt	Belgian consulting electronics engineer with unusual other interests
Jake	Owns the Pop Shop in Luxembourg City. British special agent
Jean and Marguerite Latour	Owners of hotel in Vianden and local British agents
Paul Schengen	Art expert and connoisseur, author and photographer, owner of Les Pins in Vianden
Albert	His manservant
Maria	His secretary
Rosina Conway	Simon's fiancée
Charles and Kate Hand	Married friends of Simon and Rosina

1

Man in a Tweed Hat

On a peaceful Friday afternoon in early April, Marston Baines, writer of popular thrillers, was working at his desk in his cottage in the heart of the Sussex Downs. One hour and fifty minutes later he was slumped unconscious in a helicopter flying east. He had been kidnapped.

This was the way of it.

Marston led a double life. Although a genuine and successful professional writer, he was also a special agent of the British Secret Service. A bachelor in his fifties, he lived alone and was now near retirement after many years of valuable service to his country. There was nothing special to remember about his appearance. Stoutish but loosely built. Clean-shaven and balding. Untidy conventional dress. When reading, or at his typewriter, he wore old-fashioned horn-rimmed spectacles halfway down his nose, but when he took them off his eyes were surprisingly bright and keen. He was liked and accepted in the village of Willingate. He supported the local Cricket Club and the Church Fête, enjoyed a beer or two in the evening at the Lion with the locals and was always ready to help a good cause. Mrs Brown, the widow next door who kept his cottage clean and sometimes cooked for him when he entertained friends from London, would never hear a word against him. Nor would she gossip about the hours he spent tapping away at his typewriter and throwing scrumpled balls of paper on the floor. And if he wanted to take long walks up on the hill with some of his friends that was his business. And whenever he went away on one of his foreign trips he never forgot her and sent her a coloured postcard which she proudly added to her collection pinned round her fireplace. Not surprisingly Marston thought the world of her. She never asked questions, never disturbed his papers when dusting and, so far as he knew, never told anybody that she had never seen the inside of the attic under the eaves because the door was always locked. She accepted this as one of the many peculiarities of a writer who always 'behaved like a gentleman' to her.

But on this particular April afternoon, Marston was not feeling good-tempered. He set himself to write at least two thousand words a day, but spring was in the air, he hated what he had typed and longed to be out on the hill before the gentle sunshine faded into evening.

From his desk he could see the clumps of primroses in his front garden and, as he ripped the half-typed sheet from his machine, he heard the click of the latch of the front gate.

The man who closed it carefully and then stood back to look at the house was a stranger. Marston, particularly in the summer, was used to people who stopped and stared at the cottage of the famous writer. A few knocked on his door and asked if they might thank him personally for the pleasure he had given them. A very few thrust autograph books at him.

Marston, like most writers, thrived on a little flattery. He was a keen observer of his fellow humans, and it was his habit to record the appearance, manners and speech of some visitors for future reference. This he did on a pocket tape-recorder which he kept in his sitting-room at the back of the cottage. Now he stepped back into the room so that the man would not be able to see him while he was under observation.

Marston at once surmised that his visitor was not British. Probably in his early forties but dressed in rather too obvious country tweeds and wearing a basin-shaped tweed hat that seemed out of place. Sometimes in summer, motor-coaches from Sussex coast resorts brought loads of visitors on a tour of the Downs villages and stopped for a quarter of an hour in Willingate, but April was too early. And if this man had come in a car he had left it elsewhere.

Marston sighed as he watched him come slowly up the garden path. Then, as the bell gave its usual inadequate tinkle, he put the cover on his typewriter and went to open the door.

His visitor swept off the hat with a gallant gesture and held out his other hand.

'Forgive, dear sir, this intrusion without a warning. You are, I see at once, the famous Marston Baines whose work I have admired for many years. I beg that I do not intrude nor interfere, but if I might speak with you for a while about your books it would be more than a pleasure. I wish you to know how much I and many of my friends admire not only your work but the ideas you express so clearly … Permit, dear sir, that I introduce myself. I am from Belgium. My name is Jan Schmidt. I am an electronics expert now in Eastbourne attending conference.'

Marston winced as his hand was wrung enthusiastically. 'Thank you, Herr Schmidt. I confess to Marston Baines and it is my real name. I have finished an unsatisfactory day's work and perhaps you will share a cup of tea with me and tell me about your country. Are the Ardennes as beautiful as usual? How have you found me? Where is your car?'

Schmidt left his hat on the hall table and preceded Marston into the study. After a few exaggerated exclamations of delight at the shelves of books round the room, he explained that in Marston's 'brief biography' which was printed on the jackets of his books with a photograph of the author, it was stated that he lived in Sussex.

'I have a great liking and admiration for the British countryside, Mr Baines. This is not my first visit to England, but when I realized from the map that Willingate is not far from Eastbourne I determined to try to see you ... No, Mr Baines. I do not bring my car to England for so short a visit. I have the business conference in the mornings, but to find you I come on the bus. It is easier to see the countryside when one is not driving a car ... I had hoped that you might spare a little time to tell me about the ancient green hills you call the Downs ... This is strange to me because they rise *up* from the sea and across this beautiful countryside and do not fall down ... But forgive if I make a silly joke. It is your work that interests me and many of my friends.'

Marston nodded gloomily. He wondered whether Schmidt might soon confess to an ambition to be a writer and ask for advice but mercifully this did not happen. Instead, Marston soon realized that his visitor really had made an analytical study of his work. Some of his observations were acute. For instance—

'Your skill as a storyteller has been acclaimed for years, Mr Baines. Your inside knowledge of the police, and the underworld, of spies and counter spies are obvious to any intelligent reader but I, and many of my friends, are impressed by something much more important.'

Marston raised his eyebrows. Schmidt was now speaking like an Englishman with only a trace of an accent.

'You flatter me, Mr Schmidt. What do you really want from me?'

'I would like to be sure that you share the same beliefs so often expressed in your books, Mr Baines. Forgive if this seems impertinent, but I feel sure that you must be one of those who are opposed to all forms of tyranny. I believe you have a deep hatred of all forms of persecution and intolerance and a belief in the freedom of the individual. Is that not so?'

Marston tried not to show his surprise.

'I am a storyteller, sir. Words are my business.'

'And so are ideas, Mr Baines … I fear I have offended you and ask your pardon … There are many today who share your faith in the making of a new world which is not shaped by out-of-date political ideas and dogmas. I have for long wanted to meet you. You have great gifts of persuasion and I, and a few friends, would like to ask your advice … But if I offend I will go. I had hoped that perhaps, if you are not too busy, that we could walk and talk together on your Downs …'

'Sit down, Mr Schmidt. I am not offended. We will enjoy a cup of tea together and either here, or on the hill, you shall tell me your real reason for coming to see me. Please examine my books if you would care to.' Marston was intrigued. There was surely something out of the ordinary about this man and while the kettle was boiling he went into the sitting-room and spoke softly into his pocket tape-recorder. When he carried the tray into the study Schmidt was standing by the mantelpiece with an engraved invitation card in his hand.

'Forgive again,' he said excitedly. 'I could not help seeing it. What a splendid opportunity for you to meet this most important man Paul Schengen. I know his work well. Very fine photographer and writer. He is much spoken of in my country, Mr Baines. And of course this reception for him is in London tomorrow evening. I should have been so very happy to meet him. Perhaps you already know him?'

Marston put the card back on the mantelpiece. 'No,' he said shortly, 'I have never met him. As you see, the reception is given by the Pendent Press who are also my publishers. What sort of man is Paul Schengen? Has he written and illustrated many books?'

'I am not sure,' Schmidt admitted. 'He is, I think, what you call an eccentric. Very wealthy and lives in a castle in Luxembourg. It would indeed have been lucky for me if I could have met him, as well as my favourite writer, while I am in England. I am fascinated by the business of writers and artists and publishers, Mr Baines. I am honoured to meet you today.'

His last, rather trite words, were almost drowned by the roar of a helicopter passing low over the village.

Schmidt put down his cup and walked to the window. 'For spraying the fields perhaps?' he suggested. 'In my country too they do this but are the nuisance with the noise … Forgive, Mr Baines, but I think I hear the bell of your door.'

Marston nodded his thanks, but there was nobody there. When he returned and finished his tea, Schmidt suggested that while the light was good enough they might take the promised walk and for a moment or two Marston sensed that he was now anxious to go.

As they walked up the hill together, Schmidt talked, intelligently about the Sussex countryside and when they were high enough to look across to the sea Marston, who never tired of this view, reminded his visitor that it was from some such vantage point that Britain's Charles II, on his way to exile, reined in his horse and said, 'Yes. This is a land worth fighting for.'

Schmidt nodded and turned his back on the view. 'Yes, sir. It is worth fighting for and so are some other countries. Because a few of us are sure that *you* can help us to make a new world worth fighting for, I have a most important proposition to put to you … No, sir. Please listen to me … Let us walk a little further to the wood at the top of the hill. You have knowledge and experience which is invaluable to a growing group of influential people who, without any definite political loyalties, are sure that Western civilization is decaying. You, Mr Marston Baines, are destined for the most important work of your life.'

Marston was now certainly interested in his visitor but tried to laugh off the last ridiculous suggestion. 'You're mistaken, Schmidt. I'm only a moderately successful writer looking forward to retirement. I have no influence even over my readers. I cannot change their loyalties.'

'But you can and do. Anyone who reads your books knows

that you want to preserve the best of the old world—particularly personal freedom.'

'That may be, but my house and my work are here—in this corner of England.'

'But your world is bigger than little Britain. You are often in other countries and write about them. You speak other languages. I represent those who can use your talents as they have never before been used and rewarded ... Tell me something, Mr Baines. Your last thriller was set in Brussels now called the capital of Europe. You know it well and proved it in the opening pages of your exciting story. But before the first chapter you printed an unforgettable sentence from a great English statesman. I remember it well. Do you believe that what Edmund Burke said in 1795 is still true? Let me remind you. He said, "The only thing necessary for the triumph of evil is that good men should do nothing." Do you believe that?'

Marston nodded. Suddenly he realized that he had been fooled and drugged.

'I was sure you did. A few more steps only, Mr Baines. I have a friend and colleague waiting for us in the wood. He needs your help. So do I and so do many others.' Schmidt grasped Marston's arm firmly and led him forward. Another man with tinted goggles disguising his face and wearing a black leather jacket stepped from behind a tree. One hand stayed in his pocket. In that moment Marston remembered that he had other duties and responsibilities besides those of a professional writer. Somehow he must go through with this.

He stumbled and turned to Schmidt.

'Is this your friend who is in need of my help?'

'No. This man will help us on our journey.'

'Then tell him to lead the way and to leave his gun in his pocket. He will not need it.'

Five minutes later the helicopter rose into the evening sky.

2

Peter's Party

On the morning following Marston's abduction Peter Pendent and his wife Elizabeth were together in the living room of their beautiful flat in London's district of Mayfair. The floors below were used as the offices and headquarters of their firm, known as the Pendent Press. While Marston Baines was near the end of his double life as author and secret agent, Peter was now firmly established as a professional publisher and an expert on counter-espionage. When Marston retired from the service in a few months, his books would still be published by this famous firm, but his responsibilities to his country would be over.

The two men were completely different in appearance. Marston was invariably shabby and had no interest in his clothes. Although his wits were sharp and his brain keen, he was slow in speech. Pendent, at least fifteen years younger, was smart, handsome, bearded and always dressed in the height of male fashion. He was an artistic, colourful extrovert in his publishing life, but as cool and determined in his fight against the forces of evil as Marston. The two men were good friends in spite of the difference in their ages. The elder knew that Peter would soon be taking his place, and was glad that his nephew Simon was not only a member of the Pendent Press editorial staff but was being trained by Peter as a secret agent and under his orders. Simon indeed was the only employee who knew of Peter's other life, with the exception of his wife Elizabeth who acted as his secretary.

Nine o'clock was striking as Peter walked over to the window and looked down into the street.

'As soon as we've seen the mail I must brief Simon. He's done good work on this book of Schengen's, but he must know more of our suspicions. We'll be on dangerous ground tonight ... Everything OK for the party? Of course it is. You never let me down, do you?'

'Yes, everything is in order. Peter? You *are* quite certain about Simon, aren't you? Sometimes I think you're a little rough with him. Do you like him?'

'That's not much to do with it, but the answer to your question is yes. Occasionally I wonder whether good old Marston was tough enough with him, but his record is good and our superiors are satisfied. They had their eye on him when he was up at Oxford. His languages are first class and he has done some good jobs with Marston ... I have wondered whether success came to him too soon. In a way it was awkward that his jobs so far were concerned with his uncle. Simon must get used to doing without him. I'm uneasy about tonight and Schengen, Liz. We must find out what he's really up to at that odd place of his in Luxembourg. There have been unsavoury stories about it. Hints about black magic ... Tell me, Liz. You're shrewd about people. What do you think about Marston? Is he really past it? And Simon is our responsibility now. Is he going to be a match for Schengen? Dare we risk sending him to Luxembourg?'

'Of course—if you give him your confidence. And don't compare him with Marston, who is unique and old in experience rather than years. Perhaps one day he will be persuaded to write his own story, and if he tells the truth in his usual modest way, even you, with your suspicious mind, will realize he is one of the bravest, cool-headed operators the Service has ever had. His strength is that he knows the difference between right and wrong. I'm sure he has tested Simon and has no doubts. Neither will you if you give him this chance. He'll work with you for us all as he did with Marston.'

'But he's so young, Liz. And there's this girl of his.'

'She's been involved in some of their exploits. I like her. Marston has told them both that marriage is a luxury they may not be able to enjoy, but we're married aren't we? Give him his chance with Schengen, but if you have any more doubts after you've seen Simon, have another talk with Marston tonight. The guest room is ready for him.'

Peter kissed her.

'Even if we weren't married I couldn't do without you—even as a secretary.'

'No, I don't think you could,' Elizabeth smiled. 'Like most men you tend to underestimate the intelligence and sense of purpose of women in our special line of business. You're now suspicious of Simon's girl Rosina Conway and think she may let him, and us, down when the crunch comes. I've taken the opportunity of getting to know her better and also asked Marston about her. You probably think that he's an old bachelor with a soft spot for a pretty girl, but he has seen her in action and has a very high opinion of Rosina. Simon has always been straightforward with us about her, but he has a conscience about neglecting her when they are married. I want you to know, Peter—and you must take my word for it—that she is very much tougher than she looks. A week or so ago when we knew that Schengen was coming over and that Simon was to be given the job of further investigation, you will remember that he asked if he might invite Rosina and the young married couple who are their friends and who Marston knows. You agreed and then I had my idea of asking Rosina to be of practical help at the party … We don't know Schengen personally but we can be sure that he's susceptible to flattery and that is one reason why Simon has been given this job … So I thought—'

'You wicked woman,' Peter laughed. 'You thought that the beautiful Rosina might help to impress Schengen. What have you asked her to do? And does Simon know?'

'Not yet. They are lunching together today but I don't think she'll tell him … No, Peter. All I have asked her to do is to wear the Luxembourg national costume which the women wear at certain festivals and to help by serving the Luxembourg wines. The dress is very becoming and I know that Rosina will look gorgeous. She will be introduced as Simon's fiancée and whatever Schengen may be up to he's not likely to think that Simon, a clever young editor being trained by you, and engaged to a lovely girl like Rosina, is likely to be involved in counter espionage … Rosina loved the idea and accepted at once as an opportunity to help Simon in his job. The girl cannot possibly come to any harm, but I don't think you should mention my plot to Simon when you see him presently. Let her deal with him. The caterers are sending two waitresses but they won't be in costume. It's almost as if Rosina is part of Pendent Press. She is, in a way, isn't she? … Don't you think I've been rather clever, darling?'

'Cunning is the word, Liz. Up to you now to make it work, but I don't know what Marston will think of you.'

Half an hour later Simon Baines was summoned to his office. He was a pleasant-looking young man with a long, narrow, clean-shaven face, steady grey eyes and fairish hair which he kept reasonably short.

Peter smiled a welcome. 'Good morning, Simon. I want a word with you about Schengen, his book and the party tonight. Sit down.'

'Good morning, sir. I hoped that you would find time to brief me. I've brought his file.'

Although Peter had not admitted as much to his wife, he was anxious for Simon to be a success. He knew now that the boy's easy-going, almost gentle, casual approach to everyone he met was entirely deceptive. He was aware also that Simon was much shrewder than his appearance suggested.

'Your file will not give you the sort of information we want about this man, Simon. Tonight's party will, I hope, give you the opportunity to get to know him better. I am well satisfied with your editorial work on this book. You've made a splendid job of it, and we know he is pleased with what you've done. We shall have a publishing success with *The Delectable Duchy*. The title was yours, was it not? ... Good. You've never met the man, but what have you learned about him in correspondence?'

'Brilliant photographer. An artist with words as well. Likes to be known as a way-out intellectual. Very vain and I should guess has some odd friends and hobbies ... I shall be amused to meet him tonight and see if I'm right. Once or twice he has suggested in letters that I should go and see him at this odd place he runs in Vianden ... But I told you about this, sir. You're not sure of him, are you—I mean apart from the book? What do you want me to do?'

'Forget the book, but remember that you are the only member of the staff of this publishing house who knows why we are both here. Now for Paul Schengen. I invited him to write this book on advice from above. We are suspicious of him and I will tell you why and what we expect of you tonight ... Make a fuss of him. Your analysis of him fits in with the views of the man we have watching him in Luxembourg. You remember Schengen's address? A house called Les Pins outside a small but attractive town called Vianden, almost right on the German border of Luxembourg. There are several odd things about this house. First, it is almost part of the ruins of an ancient castle on the top of a high hill above the town. Apparently Schengen, who does not seem to be married, runs Les Pins as a sort of private guest house combined with an avant-garde art gallery. He frequently has 'private views' to which the élite of the art world of Luxembourg and Belgium are invited. There are rumours that many of these exhibits are scandalous and suggestions that black magic is practised there. He travels widely and is well known amongst the intellectual smart set in Brussels. We have a good man there too, and know that Schengen is always interested in meeting officials of NATO and the EEC—particularly our countrymen known as the Brits. You should know that Brussels is now called the capital of Europe, and there is consequently a considerable social round in this now international city. We have no proof yet that he is acting for the KGB, but I am suspicious. He is exactly the sort of man they employ to recruit fanatical fellow-travellers who will work in NATO countries to undermine society, break down established standards of morality, and foment industrial unrest. You have worked with Marston and will know what efforts they are making to recruit the young. You are aware of what we are fighting.'

'Yes, I am, sir,' Simon said shortly. 'Nobody who has had the privilege of working with my uncle could have any doubts.'

'Quite so. Remember that when Marston comes here tonight, he comes only as one of our distinguished authors. We shall have no opportunity of mutual discussion and I charge you now not to attempt any other approach than that of an editorial assistant employed by his publisher. There is to be no talk of anything except books and you are to concentrate on Schengen. I expect you to persuade him to invite you to Vianden. Chat with him as much as you like. You suggested that he is vain, so flatter him. Make a fuss of him and when the opportunity occurs suggest in a subtle way that you are far from satisfied in working for me, and when the time comes you may suggest how much you dislike the present social order … Very well, Simon. You're smiling at my lecture, but I know that I can leave it to you. Now tell me about these young guests of yours this evening … Yes, we know about your Rosina. Elizabeth, as I do, thinks she will be crazy to marry you … Calm down! We know that she thinks she is prepared to run the risk but we still believe you will be more vulnerable when you are married.'

Simon grinned cheerfully.

'I know that Rosina is looking forward to meeting you and Mrs Pendent tonight, sir. You are both an example to us all. I've always thought that the opposition would be sure that a young British Agent would never be allowed to marry. The friends I'm bringing tonight are Charles Hand and his wife Kate. They were both at Oxford with me and Charles is now a teacher. Marston knows them well and approves. They've been involved with us twice. They live now in Hertfordshire and Rosina is staying with them. I'm obliged to you both for allowing me to ask them.'

'No need to get huffy, Simon. We know what you and your young friends have done in the past, but what has happened does not affect us now. I'm sure that we can trust Mr and Mrs Hand, but it would be advisable not to tell them of our suspicions of Paul Schengen. Allow them to reach their own conclusions … And Simon, don't take it badly if I remind you that this Schengen assignment is a great chance for you. I'm backing you and we'll talk again tomorrow after you've met the brilliant Paul and formed your own opinion.'

'Of course, sir. And it will be worth getting Marston's views too. Does he know about Schengen?'

'Yes. He's aware of most of our problems, but you must realize that he's on his last lap, and as I told you just now, you must not discuss tonight anything but the publishing business. Because the Pendent Press is Marston's publisher you are lucky enough to have a job here … And now get everything ready to flatter the author of *The Delectable Duchy*. We must put on a good show tonight and you have got to be Schengen's blue-eyed boy … Good luck. See you at eight o'clock. I'm meeting our guest of honour at Heathrow and taking him to the Ritz this afternoon.'

Simon went about his duties rather half-heartedly for the rest of the morning. He liked and admired his employer and enjoyed the publishing experience, but until a few months ago he had been directly under the control of Marston in his training. Now the situation was changing, and he did not like the rather subtle way in which Pendent tended to dismiss Marston as somebody who was no longer important. 'Getting old in fact and near retirement. Very good in his prime no doubt, but past it now.' It was hardly possible that Peter Pendent could be jealous of Marston Baines. He could not be as small as that, but Simon was nagged by the suspicion that his employer did not want Marston involved in this new situation. Already he knew that the Service for which he was still being tested was tough and ruthless, with no time nor money wasted on backing failures. But surely Marston had never failed and there was no evidence that the two men were not getting on well together? And Marston had always spoken highly of Peter and told Simon how lucky he was to work under him.

But he soon forgot these doubts as he settled down to his morning's work in his office and remembered that he was taking Rosina to lunch in two hours' time. She was coming direct to London by train from her parents' home in Warwickshire and then going out to Hertfordshire to spend a few nights with Charles and Kate Hand and seeing Simon every day. That indeed was the plan but he did not know how long Schengen would be in London.

Simon had first met Rosina in the little town of Fiesole outside Florence and it was there that they had both learned to love Italy. For that reason they had arranged to lunch at a famous Italian *trattoria* in the West End. They arranged to meet there at a quarter to one and Simon, sitting at the table in the window which he had reserved, was fuming with anxiety and impatience when the clock struck one. It was only a fortnight since he had spent the weekend at her home, but they were much in love and he missed her badly. He was worried too by what Peter had said to him this morning about marriage and had awful doubts as to whether he had any right to involve her in his chosen career.

Then suddenly she was there. Struggling to drag a suitcase out

47

of the taxi, laughing at the driver as he got out to help her and then blushing with pleasure when she saw Simon hurrying out to help. She was a beautiful girl. Gleaming fair hair falling to her shoulders and parted low on the right side of her head, dark eyes and a lovely figure.

'Hullo darling. How nice of you to be waiting for me. This clever driver knew this place and that's why I'm early … Thank you *so* much for looking after me and there needn't be any change.'

The driver winked at Simon. 'Thank you very much, miss. Take care of her, mate …'

Simon wisely refrained from comment on her early arrival but groaned as he lifted her suitcase.

'Please don't make a fuss in the street, Simon. The country girl has come to town prepared for every eventuality. Perhaps I forgot to tell you that I'm going to an important party tonight. And of course I've brought presents for Charles and Kate.'

They had a splendid lunch in the crowded restaurant, seeing nobody but each other. Rosina delighted the waiters by speaking to them in Italian but was quick to notice that Simon was not his usual amusing self and so, over their coffee, she took control.

'You're worried, darling. I suppose it's this party. You told me about the man from Luxembourg but you're pleased with the book, aren't you, and he's pleased with you? And what about your decorative boss, Peter? He's satisfied, I hope. You know, Simon, I like Elizabeth much more than her husband … And what about dear Marston? I'm longing to see him again. I think I should tell you, Simon, that Elizabeth wrote and asked me to do something special for them, and you, to please this man Schengen tonight … No. Don't look so furious. It's nothing shameful, but it is obvious that the three of you are dead keen to impress this man. You don't have to explain *why* he is so important to you. I promised you never to ask questions about your work and I've never broken that promise. We've helped Marston together more than once. He trusts me and what I'm going to do tonight is to help Elizabeth with this party by being a sort of assistant hostess. You ought to be proud of me instead of sulky … Sometimes, Simon, you behave like a spoiled little boy. I was going to tell you what I'm going to wear tonight but now you can wait and see.'

Simon had the grace to feel ashamed and said so, but he could not tell her now that he had been ordered to ingratiate himself with Schengen and so get an invitation to Vianden. The least that Peter could have done would surely have been to hint that Rosina had been asked to help at the party. And then it occurred to him that Peter did not know he was meeting Rosina for lunch so probably neither he, nor Elizabeth, would mention it before the party. So he tried not to show his annoyance as he took Rosina back to St. Pancras station in a taxi.

She kissed him affectionately before he left for the office.

'Thank you for a lovely lunch, darling. Charles will meet me in the car at St Albans and we'll all three be at Pendents before eight o'clock. It will be wonderful when this party is over and I hope Peter will give you a few days off so that we can have some time together before I go home … I'll ask him, Simon. I'm doing this thing for Elizabeth tonight and it's the least they can do for us … I hope you'll be proud of me when you see me this evening … No, I'm not going to tell you now. I want it to be a surprise. Don't be cross with me any more, dear Simon.'

There was not much to do when he got back to the office. The magnificent room on the first floor which the Pendents used as a showroom for their publications was being transformed into an elegant salon by the caterers. On the wall above the buffet at the far end was the Luxembourg flag of red, white and blue horizontal stripes, and gracing the other panelled walls were enlargements of Schengen's photographs which illustrated his book. Simon, who had chosen the pictures and seen them many times stopped in front of the most dramatic of them all—a picture of the mighty Château Vianden on the wooded hilltop above the town. He remembered that parts of this were tenth and eleventh century and that some Roman remains had been found on the site. He recalled also that Peter, in his briefing this morning, had mentioned that Schengen's house called Les Pins was built close to the ruins although the author never mentioned this in the book. And there were hints of unusual goings-on in the home of this remarkable man.

'Yes, Simon,' Peter's familiar voice spoke behind him. 'It is a magnificent picture and I congratulate you again on the book ... You'll make a good editor.'

'Thank you, sir. I've enjoyed working on it.' He looked round and when he realized that nobody was in the room except his employer, he added, 'I was wondering why Schengen should want to live right up against the walls of that fantastic place.'

'That's what I want you to find out ... I believe this man is too much of a show-off to be true. We shall know more tonight. I'm glad Marston will be here. And Simon, Elizabeth tells me that your Rosina has promised to help her as a sort of assistant hostess tonight. We like your girl, and no doubt she'll tell you later what she thinks of our guest. One other point. While we're on the publishing job, I'm Peter to you and all my staff—not "sir". Good luck, Simon. You can clear off now if there's nothing else you can do here. See you about seven thirty.'

And that was that, so Simon returned thoughtfully to his small flat to bath and change and by the time he was back again he had recovered his usual good spirits. Before he could open the door, the tooting of a car's horn announced the arrival of the Hands and Rosina.

'Look after these lovelies while I find a place to park,' Charles grinned. 'If your party tonight is half as noisy as the gossiping of these two behind me I shan't be able to make myself agreeable to your other guests … Don't worry about me. I'll let myself in.'

Charles Hand was shorter than Simon, red-haired and wore spectacles. Academically clever, even before he went to Oxford he was determined to teach, which he was now doing to the sixth form of a comprehensive school in Hertfordshire. He had first met golden-haired Kate at university and helped to save her life and reason in one of their adventures with Marston Baines in Provence. Behind a flippant manner which was often misunderstood, Charles was dedicated to his belief that it was his own generation that could do much to make a better world. He had a great admiration for Marston Baines, who had once pointed out that tolerance is often used as an excuse for evil doing, and that what you believe to be right is worth fighting for. He had been married to his beautiful Kate for only eighteen months and had never been so happy in his life.

Simon told him where to park and then, on the doorstep of the Pendent Press, the two girls kissed him and Kate said, 'Will we do, Simon? Rosina has been telling us about the Pendents and your wonderful job that this party is all about … You haven't seen her dress yet, have you? Show him, Rosie.'

Only Kate was allowed to call her Rosie. She was wearing a long black velvet cloak and felt a little shy as she grabbed Simon's hand. 'Of course I'll show him, but not on the pavement. Please take me to Elizabeth first, darling … I was only teasing you at lunchtime. It's not all that special. It was Elizabeth's idea. She got it for me.'

Elizabeth was waiting for her guests at the top of the stairs and greeted the girls warmly. 'Thank you for bringing them early, Simon. Everything is going well. Peter will soon be down with Schengen. He's quite a character. You girls come and tidy up. How's the dress, Rosina?'

Rosina flashed Simon a smile and was parted from him again for ten minutes.

The big room looked superb. Two waiters in white coats behind the buffet were lighting candles and an electrician had adjusted the overhead lighting so that the photographs round the walls were skilfully illuminated. The curtains were drawn and the tables on each side of the room were lit by shaded candles. Simon was nervous. He knew that much was expected of him this evening and this was a very special party. Amongst the guests would be dignitaries from the Luxembourg Embassy, journalists from newspapers, famous photographers, and some friends of Peter and Elizabeth, some of whom would be other publishers and, of course, authors and artists whose work was published by the firm.

It would be good to see Marston again. Simon knew that his uncle hated smart parties but that he would be here to meet Paul Schengen for reasons unconnected with publishing, and which he had promised not to mention or discuss. It was going to be a tricky evening and he was suddenly aware that Rosina's presence was going to help. He'd been a fool to fuss about her secret with Elizabeth which was obviously a very special dress.

Then he heard Charles speaking to a girl from the caterers who was showing the guests where to leave their coats, but before he could go down to him his own name was called from the door at the other end of the room.

'Simon, come and meet our special guest,' Peter Pendent called. 'He's been asking for you and has already met Rosina.'

Simon never forgot that first vital meeting—the prelude to the most dramatic adventure of his young life. A few paces behind Peter and Elizabeth was Paul Schengen with his fingers on Rosina's arm. Never had he seen Rosina look more beautiful. As she caught his glance she moved away from Schengen and then, in response to a ripple of applause, she smilingly dropped a curtsey to the guests as Simon hurried across to her. She looked lovely in a crimson, short-sleeved dress worn over a white blouse with long sleeves. Tied round her waist was a white apron with a gaily coloured embroidered border. Her hair was covered by a pleated, white muslin bonnet. Her stockings were white and her shoes black.

Later he learned that this was the traditional dress worn by Luxembourg girls at special festivals such as wine harvests and folk dances. Elizabeth had discovered it and asked Rosina to wear it as a compliment to their special guest, and with a stab of jealousy Simon realized that Schengen was already appreciating the gesture.

But he quickly recovered his poise and after shaking hands concentrated on the main task of the evening, which was to make himself agreeable to this important visitor. Schengen was shorter than he expected. Clean-shaven, but with a head of dark red wavy hair. Behind steel-framed spectacles his eyes were keen and grey.

'My dear fellow,' he said, without a trace of accent. 'It is indeed a pleasure to meet you and to congratulate and thank you for all the intelligent help and advice you have given me over our book. I am honoured tonight in many ways. This party in the gracious house of my London publisher. The hospitality of my host and hostess, and the altogether charming welcome given to me by the prettiest girl I am likely to see in England wearing the traditional dress of my own little country. Miss Conway has already told me that you are affianced and I trust you will accept my congratulations.'

He turned to bow to Rosina, who took this opportunity to wink at her affianced and then shook hands again. His clasp was soft and damp and Simon smiled his thanks not caring much for the effusive comments.

But he was soon to realize that this man had a compulsive personality. He mixed easily with the other guests and was charming to Charles and Kate when Simon presented them as two old friends. Rosina who, by now, was helping to serve the light, white wines of Luxembourg, tactfully asked him if he approved of their choice, and then said, 'I know Simon is looking forward to introducing you to his uncle Marston Baines. I'm sure you have heard of his work and as he is published by Pendents he was one of the authors specially invited to meet you. Has he arrived yet, Simon? You know how Kate and I adore him and I'm longing to ply him with wine.'

'But of course I want to meet him. I admire his work very much and for years have looked forward to exchanging ideas with him. He is a famous and experienced writer and I shall value his opinion on our book, Simon … I may call you Simon now that we have met, may I not? Will you, if you please, take me to him?'

The room was nearly full now but Simon could not see his uncle. Charles and Kate admitted that they had been hopefully looking for him, but at that moment two press photographers arrived, and Simon had no difficulty in persuading Schengen to pose in front of the display of *The Delectable Duchy*. Several pictures were taken, including one with Rosina at his side, another with Peter and Elizabeth and another with Simon.

The atmosphere thickened and the select party grew noisier. Peter beckoned to Simon and asked him if he knew why Marston had not turned up.

'Not like him, Simon. I know he intended to be here. Nip up to my office and ring the cottage.'

Only Rosina noticed him leave the room and followed him.

'You're worried about Marston, Simon. So is Elizabeth. She asked me twice if I'd seen him. Perhaps he's had an accident? Maybe he's too injured to telephone and the police wouldn't know he was due here.'

Simon nodded and was even more anxious when he had twice telephoned Marston's cottage without success.

'Don't let the others see we're fussed,' he said. 'I must tell Peter there's no reply and we must decide what to say to Schengen … You don't care for that man, do you?'

'No darling, I don't,' she said and kissed him quickly. 'I care for Marston, though.'

Back in the crowded room Simon managed to indicate to Peter that there was no reply from the cottage and then, remembering that he had got to ingratiate himself with Schengen, he tried to forget Marston and moved over to a small group that included Charles, Kate and Rosina. They were being entertained by the guest of honour.

'So here you are, my boy. I was missing you, but your young friends are a delightful substitute,' said Schengen. 'The photographers have gone, so we must look carefully and hopefully at tomorrow's papers. I have arranged that a selection of pictures be sent to our daily paper in Luxembourg ... Ah, here is our hostess. I was just telling these young people how much I have been looking forward to meeting the famous Marston Baines. I fear he has been delayed.'

Elizabeth flicked Simon a warning glance.

'Yes, Paul. I'm sorry we did not tell you earlier but both of us thought the other had conveyed his apologies to you. Forgive us. Marston telephoned late this afternoon. He was very upset not to meet you, but he has been called to hospital to visit a Sussex friend who has been gravely injured in a car accident. We'll arrange a special meeting next time you come over, and Peter and I hope that will be soon. We're sure that now *The Delectable Duchy* is published there will be plenty of bookshops wanting you for signing sessions.'

This was a good enough hint to the four young people and Rosina was quick to take up her cue.

'You might have told us before, Elizabeth! Kate and I have been pining for Marston. Are you sure he didn't send us a special message? I wanted him to see me like this ... You must understand, Mr Schengen, that Marston Baines is practically my uncle by marriage and we have much in common—Simon, for instance ... Excuse me now, if you please, but I must be about my duties.' As Elizabeth took her arm she looked back and her smile was for the guest of honour.

As Charles and Kate drifted away Schengen turned to Simon.

'You are a very fortunate young man. I congratulate you again, Simon—and not only on your charming Miss Conway but on your work here. I am impressed by the way in which the Pendent Press has presented my book tonight. I hope we shall get to know each other better, Simon ... Another book perhaps? It is a pleasure to work with an organization so sympathetic towards the ideals of youth and to new ideas and so skilled in presenting them ... I should like you to come and see me in Luxembourg, Simon. And to bring Miss Conway, of course. You must both come.'

Simon was suspicious. Why should Schengen react like this so quickly? Possibly he was attracted by Rosina. Most men were, but why, after only about two hours' acquaintance, should he be invited to visit him in Luxembourg when this was precisely what Pendent expected of him?

'This is very kind of you, sir. May I say how much I have enjoyed meeting you tonight. I am fascinated by your book and grateful for your interest in me and my work. Indeed, I have decided to ask your advice on a personal matter, but can hardly do so now. In a few minutes the other guests will be going and wish to say goodbye to you. Perhaps I could have a word tomorrow, but if that is not convenient be sure I would be happy to come to Vianden. And Rosina will be thrilled. I have some holiday due and it would be marvellous to see Les Pins.'

'That is good, Simon. We will arrange it, but not tomorrow. And you are right about my duties now. I think Mr Pendent is a little anxious ... Tell me in confidence. Are you happy and satisfied with your job here? It is important for me to know.'

'Yes, sir. Happy enough, but as Rosina has promised to marry me in the summer I must get a better job. She agrees that we must have more money than this small firm can afford. There are a few other factors also.'

'She is probably right, Simon. I may be able to help. Tell her now about my invitation and we will speak again before I leave.'

Simon did not have the opportunity to tell her much as the party began to break up, but when Schengen's car was announced he left the group he was with and crossed the room to them, and Rosina thanked him warmly for his invitation.

'I hope you will come, my dear. It has been a great pleasure to meet you and I feel sure that you will both respond to the atmosphere of Les Pins. As soon as I know when you can come I will arrange a special party for you. You shall meet some other artists and interesting people who may be valuable to such an intelligent and gifted young man as Simon. Les Pins is special. It is only for the artist, the creator, the intellectual, the specialist—indeed I have created it for the young in heart as well as the young in mind who wish to sweep away all old ideas and ways of living. I hope you will come—indeed, I expect you to do so. Neither of you will regret it.'

He bent over Rosina's hand and kissed it and before Simon could comment, Charles and Kate came over and asked if there was any news of Marston.

'Peculiar sort of party, Simon,' Charles added. 'I didn't know your boss went in for this sort of thing but your tame author seems to like you both and I suppose that's good for business.'

'Never mind about that,' Simon snapped. 'You two stay around, please, until we've got some news of Marston. He may have got another message through.'

At last the four young people were alone with Elizabeth and Peter.

Simon was on edge.

'Perhaps you will tell us now whether what Elizabeth told Schengen about Marston is true. I don't believe it. Has he had an accident? How do we know? It's not like him not to turn up nor to communicate.'

'Keep your cool, Simon,' Peter said. 'I've just telephoned

Marston's cottage again. There's nobody there: he did not ring us this afternoon. Elizabeth saw no sense in showing Schengen that we were worried. You've got a key to the cottage, haven't you? Good. Borrow my car and go down there now and see what you can find out. Go down the Eastbourne road the way he would have come. If there has been a serious accident on the way there will be some sign of it. I'm not keen on telephoning the police and enquiring at hospitals at this stage.'

'You would if you were asking after Marston the author,' Rosina said shrewdly. 'We're only talking about one of your important guests who didn't arrive. I'm going with Simon and we'll telephone you from the cottage as soon as we get there. If there has been an accident of course we'll ring at once. We know you're worried and so are we.'

'OK,' Peter agreed. 'We know Marston's phone is working. Don't dawdle on the way. What about your pals, Charles and Kate? I'm trusting you not to chat about Marston's disappearance.'

'We're going too,' Charles said firmly. 'More sensible that we go in my car, which is just round the corner. Kate would never have married me if it wasn't for Marston and we must keep an eye on these two. We're on holiday so it doesn't matter what time we get back tomorrow.'

3

The Message

Charles drove fast through the night with Simon beside him, and the girls dozing on the back seat. As they crossed Westminster Bridge the hands of Big Ben pointed to half past eleven. The moon came up and, as they bypassed Croydon and just before they reached East Grinstead, Charles stopped at an all-night filling station for more petrol. From a telephone box nearby, Simon again telephoned Marston's cottage, but there was no reply.

'Not really up to me to interfere,' Charles said as Simon got back into the car. 'We'll drive you anywhere you like, but aren't you taking Marston too seriously? He's a wily old bird and really is capable of looking after himself and managing his own affairs. He may have telephoned your boss by now and just been held up on the way to London. You can't be sure that he would come this way. He might have used the Brighton road.'

'If you're tired of driving I'll take over,' Simon snapped. 'You know Pendent ordered me to go to Willingate and I'm going. You offered to take us and we're obliged. This is the road Marston uses when he comes to London, and if he knew he was going to be late or prevented from coming he would have telephoned us. You should know him better. The four of us here all owe him plenty. I've had my orders and you know perfectly well, Charlieboy, that Pete doesn't want to call in the police—or take other steps—until

I've had a look round. So please shut up and drive on. Or let me do so ... Are you girls awake?'

'Don't take too much notice of my husband,' Kate murmured. 'He's a little overtired and excited. He's not used to expensive parties. Simon's right, Charles. Marston is a marked man even here in England. Maybe even in Sussex. Because he is a popular writer, almost anyone can find out where he lives. We know that he must have many political opponents who would like him eliminated. He knows too much, and many of his enemies are aware that he is also the famous writer ... Simon has been told to search the cottage because he knows it, and the village, better than any of us, or any of Marston's publishing friends. Now I'm going to sleep on Rosie's shoulder, but keep a lookout for any signs of an accident.'

Kate did not often speak out so plainly, and Charles was obviously as surprised as Simon. They apologized to each other and Charles drove on through Sussex until they saw the South Downs ahead of them outlined against the starry sky. There was not much traffic, but soon after Simon had taken over the wheel about twenty miles from Willingate a police car roared past them, pulled in to the side of the road and flashed on their 'Stop' sign.

The two officers asked them courteously where they were going and where they came from? Simon explained that they were on their way to his uncle's cottage in Willingate having come from a party in London.

'Perhaps you know about Mr Marston Baines,' Rosina broke in. 'He's an important author and he was supposed to be at this party but he didn't arrive. Can you tell us whether there has been a car accident on any of the roads to London this afternoon? We are a little worried so we're on our way to see if he's safe and sound in his cottage.'

Both policemen were obviously amused by Rosina who was, of course, still in her Luxembourg dress, but when Kate asked why they had stopped them, and were they looking for anybody special, they replied that they kept an eye on cars coming to and from the south coast at this time of night. They then returned to their car, used their radio, and came back to reassure them that no serious accident involving a scarlet Mini had been reported on any of the roads to London.

Simon thanked them and promised to telephone if they wanted help.

'My uncle has probably forgotten the London party. He's getting on a bit now and inclined to be absent-minded. Probably fast asleep and never heard the telephone … We'll let you know if we're in trouble. Goodnight—or rather good morning!'

When the police had driven off, Simon reminded the others again that it was a mistake to show how anxious they were. 'We don't want anybody else fussing round the cottage until we've searched it. Anyway we'll know in ten minutes. If Marston's car is still in his garage and he's not at home there will be every reason to start worrying. I'm sorry now that I've brought you into this, and I can't help wondering whether those two cops believed us. We don't want them turning up in Willingate … And if Marston is there now he'll take a very poor view of our interference.'

They had left the main road while Simon was talking and were in a tree-lined lane winding its leisurely way beneath the great bulk of the Downs on their right. The moon was high now and cast great splashes of shadow on the road. The beauty of the night silenced them all, and as Simon stopped the car and switched off the engine in Willingate's only street, he whispered, 'Not a sound, please, until we're inside. We mustn't wake Mrs Brown next door until we've searched the place. I've got the garage key as well and we'll look there first. Don't slam the car doors and you girls wait on the step while Charles and I look in the garage.'

The wooden shed in which Marston kept his car was in part of his front garden next to the adjoining cottage. The double doors, fastened only with a padlock, opened quietly and easily. His car was there and the doors were locked.

'So he never started,' Simon murmured. 'I don't like this, Charlieboy. Wish we hadn't brought the girls. Do you think they'll stay outside while we search the house?'

'No they won't,' Rosina whispered behind them. 'You've still got a lot to learn about women, Simon. Open the front door and we'll search the place and get it over.'

Nevertheless, she felt for his free hand as he unlocked the door of the cottage which swung back at his touch. She had been there before and switched on the light as soon as the others were inside. Within three minutes they knew that Marston was not there. His bed had not been slept in, the desk in his study was as untidy as usual, the typewriter was covered and there were several balls of paper on the floor by the waste-paper basket. Simon smoothed them out but they were only scraps of dialogue from the story Marston was working on. He knew his uncle's writing habits and there was nothing unusual about these. Charles was watching him gloomily when Kate called excitedly from the kitchen.

'Come here, Simon. Marston had a visitor. Two dirty teacups in the sink.'

This was an important clue and while they were discussing its significance they were startled by a stealthy knock on the back door. Simon noticed that the door was locked but there was no key in it. He signalled to the others to keep quiet and then, with his ear against the panel said firmly, 'Who's there? What do you want?'

A muffled voice answered.

'It's me. Martha Brown from next door. I want to know if Mr Baines come back. I'm in charge here when he's away and unless you lot say who you are I'll fetch the police.'

Simon laughed. 'Good for you, Mrs Brown. It's Simon here with some friends, and you're just the person we want. Unlock the door and come in.'

The lock clicked back to disclose a curious female figure. Mrs Brown was wearing a winter coat over a voluminous flannel nightgown. Her hair was in curlers and she had forgotten to put her teeth in, but there was no doubt that she was pleased to see Simon and Rosina, who stepped forward to welcome her.

'These are our friends, Mr and Mrs Hand,' she explained. 'We've all been to a party in London. We expected to see Mr Baines there so we just thought we'd come down and see if he's all right. We're sorry if we woke you.'

Charles smiled at Martha and pulled forward a kitchen chair for her, but it was Simon to whom she spoke.

'So he hasn't been back then? I see him go up the hill like he always does of an evening when he gets the chance. Wearing one of those round tweedy hats, he was.'

'When was this, Martha? And do you mean to say that my uncle was wearing a tweedy hat? He always wears a cap when he goes walking. Come in the study and tell us all about it. Rosina will bring us a cup of tea. We all need one.'

They settled her in an easy chair but she was not very coherent until the girls brought the tea and fussed over her.

'Now Martha,' Simon coaxed her. 'Just try to remember when you last saw my uncle and what you meant by him wearing a round tweed hat.'

'Not last evening it wasn't. Yesterday was Saturday. It were Friday then. And I didn't say as he was wearing one of them pudding basin hats. It was his friend. Stranger to the village he was. Mrs Bourn up the street sees him get off the bus and he was asking for Mr Marston Baines like they all do.'

'Like all who do?' Rosina asked. 'You see, Martha, we expected to see Mr Baines at this party in London last night. There's the invitation card on the mantelpiece. We've come down here to see why he didn't arrive. Do you know why? Did he tell you he was going to London yesterday?'

'O' course he didn't, miss. Why should he? Where he goes is no business o' mine. I keeps myself to myself in Willingate and Saturdays I never come in here to tidy up unless he asks me. But Mr Baines is a very special gentleman to me. He don't always tell me whether he's going away except if it's for a long time on one of his furrin' trips when he sends me postcards …'

'Yes, of course we understand that,' Simon broke in. 'Please try to remember that man in the tweed hat. You say he came by bus?'

'So that Mrs Bourn says. She's a nosy one. You can ask her in the morning if you like. He was asking for Marston Baines like many of these trippers from Eastbourne and Hastings and Brighton who read his books. Most of 'em come in cars, but when I was in bed on Friday I remembered that I hadn't seen him come back from his walk with that chap with the hat. Nothing to do with me, o' course, and I can't be watching from my window all the time.'

'No. Of course you can't,' Kate said promptly as she refilled the old lady's cup. 'And I expect you were too busy yesterday to notice whether Mr Baines was about. Has anybody else been asking for him?'

By now Mrs Brown was looking bewildered and very unhappy. 'Not so far as I know, midear. It must have been your car woke me just now so I gets up to see who it was at this time o' night. And when I opens my door I could see it in the moonlight and I see it wasn't Mr Simon's car and then I see Mr Simon 'cos the curtains weren't drawn proper.'

Simon signalled to Charles to follow him and closed the study door.

'I must telephone Peter at once, Charles. The phone is in the other room. Keep them all in there and don't let old Mother Brown out until I come back … Something wrong here.'

The telephone in Marston's sitting-room was on a small, antique desk under one of the windows. As he reached for the receiver, Simon noticed Marston's pocket tape-recorder in one of the pigeon-holes. He knew that his uncle used this frequently to record impressions of people he might use one day in a story, and any other ideas which might be of value when working on a book.

Simon replaced the telephone and switched on the recorder. At once Marston's unmistakable voice came to him as clearly as if he was sitting beside him:

"Must remember this smart Belgian who says his name is Jan Schmidt and is trying, but not succeeding, to dress like the traditional English gentleman. Could use a character like this. Says he is an electronics engineer at a conference in Eastbourne. Could be true. Something odd about him. Says he doesn't bring his car to England but came over here by bus. Much too flattering about the books. Overacting somewhat ... That's it. Done his homework about the books but wants something else ... Vain about his appearance. Wearing an expensive wig. Not a bad idea for a character who wants to disguise himself sometimes by leaving it off ..."

The familiar voice stopped and Simon was strangely moved. Typical Marston, but where was he now?

His hand was on the telephone again as Charles came into the room and closed the door.

'News for you. Thought you should know at once. The old dame says that a helicopter was busy over the village Friday afternoon and it went over the hill again after Marston went out with his visitor.'

4

Jan Schmidt

Marston was incapable of resistance, as with Schmidt's hand grasping his arm he stumbled across the clearing. He was dimly aware that the young man in the leather jacket helped to haul him into the waiting helicopter, and his last thought was that he had been fooled by his plausible visitor. His tea had been drugged, of course. Doctored by Schmidt when he had suggested that somebody was at the front door of the cottage.

He was never sure for how many hours he had been unconscious. Gradually he became aware of a rhythmic throbbing and a disturbing sensation of movement of whatever was supporting his body. He wondered if he was in bed and slowly opened his eyes. A moving light hanging above his head puzzled him until he realized that he was lying on the cushioned bunk of a boat at sea.

Then a familiar voice invited him to sit up and he realized that Jan Schmidt was helping him to raise himself.

'That is better, Mr Baines. There is nothing now for you to worry about. You are safe and will feel better when you have drunk this. It will not harm you. Indeed, I have just enjoyed a cup of this excellent soup myself and please notice that I am tasting from your cup now. We have a doctor aboard and when he can hand over the wheel he will reassure you and we will explain all … Meanwhile I have to apologize for any inconvenience caused …'

Marston tasted the soup and smiled ruefully. 'Thank you, Schmidt. I look forward to your explanation, but I must tell you that your last remark seems to me to be the understatement of the year. Neither my friends nor my enemies—and I'm not yet sure which you are—apologize for "inconvenience caused" after accepting my hospitality, drugging me at my own table and then kidnapping me. I demand to know who you really are, where we are going and why.'

'Very well, Mr Baines. You have a right to the answers to your questions and I will explain our motives for bringing you to Belgium in this way. I will not wait for Dr Carter, but please realize that we wish you no harm, and hope that you will believe that we, and those whom we represent, need not only your co-operation and help in our mission, but your friendship as well. We believe that you share our ideals and have knowledge and experience which will be of the greatest value to our organization. We have studied your work closely. We admire your expertise as a writer, and the way in which you present certain unpopular facts to your public and we want you on our side. Urgently.'

'And so you drugged and kidnapped me? A curious act of friendship … Help me out of this damned bunk and get on with your story.'

Marston was now clear-headed and inclined to believe that Schmidt was not an enemy. It was unlikely, but just possible, that he was aware of his true identity, and that their references to his work as a writer were a blind. His life work as a secret agent had brought him many enemies who wanted him dead, but apart from anything else Marston was convinced that it was his duty to discover Schmidt's true identity and what he was up to.

So, he listened attentively to one of the strangest statements he had ever heard as the small boat battered its way through what sounded like a very rough crossing.

'What I told you in your cottage is correct, Mr Baines. My name *is* Jan Schmidt. I am a Belgian living in the suburbs of Brussels. I am a consultant electronics engineer and I have been attending a conference in Eastbourne. That is the truth. I am now trusting you with secret information concerning a new organization. We are gaining strength every day in the western countries of Europe— particularly in those of the NATO alliance and the European Economic Community. The members of this organization are recruited from all classes but particularly from the professions and one-man businesses. We are *not* another political party but we are pledged to fight the tyranny of totalitarianism in all forms. We are not "fascists" but admit that our chief enemy is Soviet Marxism which is opposed to all personal freedom—and the gradual subjugation of Western Europe. We believe that freedom's most dangerous enemy is the great Soviet spy machine known as the KGB, and we believe, from your writings, that you too share this belief and will be willing to help us. As I said just now, we are sure that part of KGB policy is to destroy Western society from within. Their spies are everywhere. In Brussels, we know that they are in the EEC. They work on people. They corrupt. They use bribery, blackmail, seduction, drugs and black magic. Our organization believes that our Western countries, often for political reasons, are not facing up to these dangers. They are soft, and often because a few in high places are in the pay of the KGB …'

Schmidt paused and mopped his forehead.

'Very interesting,' Marston said quietly. 'Very interesting indeed. I have no doubt of your sincerity but what is all this to do with me, and why go to the trouble of abducting me? Has your organization a name?'

'We are known among ourselves as La Promesse. We are pledged to fight this tyranny. We swear to do so. At present we are not supported by any of our governments. We hope and believe that you sympathize with our aims. Your writings prove that. We have taken a chance in bringing you to Brussels in this way. We want your help and believe that Britain needs it too. We want to use your undoubted gifts as a writer to promote the beliefs and aims of La Promesse in all countries. We want recruits. We have been studying your work. I have been in England two weeks. I have been to Willingate in a hired car. I have walked alone on your hill, and found the place where the helicopter could land. I did not dare to tell you about La Promesse in your own home. I could not risk refusal. You might have asked for time to consider, but we have a meeting in my house this evening and wish you to be present to hear reports from our members. I give *you* my promise, Mr Baines, that if then you cannot help or advise us, we shall take you back to Sussex and never bother you again. We shall trust you not to disclose what I have told you or what you will learn when you meet the others. You are here now because we have little time to spare.'

Peter Pendent had once told Marston a little of the underground movement calling themselves La Promesse, but had not apparently considered it important. Nevertheless Marston was impressed by the possibilities mentioned by Schmidt and it was true that he was in personal sympathy with the new movement. Obviously it was his duty to investigate further, although it was possible, though unlikely, that these people knew that he was still a British secret agent.

'This is all very well, Schmidt. I do happen to be in sympathy with your general aims, but if there is little time to spare—and I'm not sure what you mean by this—how can I, a professional writer, help you? And why abduct me to do so?'

'I have tried to explain that you will know more after our meeting tonight, sir.'

'Very well, but tell me if your helicopter pilot would have shot me if I had refused to come with you?'

Jan smiled. 'No, Mr Baines. He had no gun and anyway the drug was working. I have used it before and its timing is reliable. That was why I paused at the top of the hill and we had the pleasant little conversation about the view. I did not wish to have to carry you to the helicopter. Please trust us, Mr Baines. We need to enlist your skills with some subtle propaganda. We have some vital information for your Government and hope you will help us to find the best way of passing this to the right quarter.'

Marston showed no surprise. Schmidt might be the idealist he professed to be, but Marston was aware that the KGB might be using La Promesse in some way to recruit new agents. He had no illusions about the world of double cross in which he had been working for most of his life, and it was possible that if he played his cards carefully he might get some important information for his superiors.

Daylight was now showing through the porthole, and as he had not turned up at Peter's party it might be that his disappearance would be known. Possibly Simon would be called in to help, but somehow or other he must report to Peter Pendent as soon as possible. And was there really an English doctor aboard?

This last question was answered when the cabin door was opened by a cheerful young man in jeans and jersey who gave him a friendly grin and a warm handshake.

'Sorry about all this, Mr Baines. Hope Jan has explained about us and that you're none the worse for your spell of amnesia ... Yes, I'm English. Name of Carter and a doctor who prefers to work out of Britain. Near neighbour of Jan and I hope you're going to come in with us ... We'll be landing in half an hour.'

'You won't get me through Belgian customs without a passport,' Marston snapped.

'But you won't need one, Mr Baines. We are not landing at a port but on private land. We left the east coast of England in the same sort of privacy and my car will be waiting for us.'

'But suppose I make a fuss and demand to see the police and tell them about the helicopter and that I have been abducted?'

'You will not do that,' Schmidt said quietly. 'We know our man. You know about us now and we're sure you're curious enough to want to know more. You will not make trouble in such an obvious way. La Promesse has many friends now in Belgium—even in the police and customs in the ports. You are an English friend of ours and our guest, and we believe you will behave as such … Now, if you will excuse, I will change into my Belgian suit, and do not show surprise if, when you see me again, I have not so much hair. In my country I do not dress like the English sportsman and do not look like the picture on my passport which I used to enter your country.'

Marston smiled to himself as he remembered how he had recorded the wig. Would Simon have the sense to look for the tape-recorder and switch it on? Almost certainly, yes.

'Very well. I'll come peacefully. A writer never misses a chance of a new experience, but I expect you to help me send a message to my friends in England to relieve their anxiety.'

'No doubt arrangements for that can be made,' the doctor smiled.

Marston was not sure whether they landed on the Belgian or Dutch coast. He was unfamiliar with the maze of inlets and waterways of the sandy coasts of the Low Countries north of Antwerp. Jan Schmidt, now in his Belgian clothes and without a wig, stayed with him in the cabin as the cruiser slipped into a narrow creek lined with pine trees. Marston heard footsteps on the deck above as the boat bumped gently against a landing stage and then Hugh Carter's invitation to come ashore.

'All quiet and a fine morning, Mr Baines. Hope the sea trip hasn't been too uncomfortable for you. Coffee and sandwiches in my car and in a few hours we'll be in Brussels.'

Jan had little to say and Marston not much time to look round as they stepped ashore. The helicopter pilot, busy on the deck, gave him a smile and Marston supposed correctly that he was not coming with them. He noticed a boat shed a few yards away and the glimpse of a pleasant house beyond the screen of trees. He glanced at his wrist and realized that his watch had stopped but guessed the time to be about 9 o'clock in the morning.

Jan took his arm and led him along a sandy track while Carter hurried ahead. Marston wondered whether they were going to the house first. They were not, and as they stepped out of the shadows of the trees he saw a large blue saloon car parked in a clearing. Carter opened the rear door.

'You will see that we are not troubled by customs formalities, Mr Baines. This house, and the boat which brought us here safely, belong to one of our many friends. We are in Holland now but shall be in Belgium soon. I hope you have not been too uncomfortable, but please refresh yourself as we travel and if you are tired after your experiences don't hesitate to sleep.'

The car was luxurious, the coffee hot and the sandwiches welcome. Jan, beside him, had little to say as Carter drove fast through flat and rather dull country, and Marston was soon drowsy. Jan, beside him, had his eyes closed, and soon he too slept for a while. Marston remembered that this was Saturday morning and that Pendent's party was not until this evening so it was possible that his abduction would not be realized for nearly twenty-four hours. Then he slept and did not waken until they were in the outskirts of Brussels. He did not know this city well, but was not surprised when Jan explained that Hugh Carter and he lived next door to each other in the woods of Uccle on the outskirts of the city. He remembered then that this attractive, but oddly named suburb, on the Waterloo side was much favoured by diplomats, civil servants and officials from the EEC, as well as the wealthier citizens who work in the international city. As Carter drove into this pleasant district, Marston realized that it was the sort of place in which an important consultant electronics engineer with a successful practice would choose to live.

The houses of the two friends were at the top of a quiet cul-de-sac, ending in the woods. Neither was pretentious, but as Marston got out of the car he remembered the windswept Downs of Sussex and wondered how anybody could live happily surrounded by trees!

'We shall meet later, Mr Baines,' Carter called from the driving seat. 'It is a privilege to have you with us, but please be patient until you have met some more of our friends this evening.'

Marston nodded and followed Schmidt up to his front door which was opened before he could get out his key by a pretty, dark woman who smiled a welcome.

'Rose, my dear, this is our English friend, the author Marston Baines, who has promised to help us … My wife is English, Mr Baines, and she knows that I have told you about La Promesse.'

'We are proud and pleased to welcome you here, Mr Baines. Jan will show you your room and then lunch will be ready.'

Marston tried not to show his surprise. There was no reason why Schmidt should not have an English wife, but he wondered if she knew whether he had been drugged and abducted.

His room was comfortable and spacious. Amongst the books on his bedside table was one of his own—a tactful gesture which suggested that he really was expected. But even more significant was an open suitcase on the foot of the bed.

'We have taken the liberty of providing you with some changes of clothing and other toilet necessities,' Jan explained. 'There was always the possibility that you would not have time to pack … No, Mr Baines. Please do not be angered … After we have eaten I will tell you more.'

The meal was pleasant and the conversation general. Mrs Schmidt was interested to hear about her husband's opinion of Eastbourne and the Sussex Downs, and spoke intelligently to Marston about his books. After coffee the two men asked to be excused and retired upstairs.

'You will be tired I am sure,' Schmidt began, 'but before you rest for a few hours before this evening's meeting I must tell you more. The situation has changed somewhat—become more urgent since yesterday when I first met you—and I must ask you now to answer one question—'

Marston lost patience.

'I am under no obligation to answer any of your questions. You have drugged and abducted me and by now I shall have been missed. I insist upon telephoning my friends and returning to England as soon as possible.'

'I do not think you will be missed until this evening when you fail to appear at Mr Pendent's party in London, and it is in connection with that social event that I want to speak to you privately before the others come. I am trusting you, Mr Baines, and I do beg you to wait a few hours before contacting England. We should not have brought you here in this way if the matter was trivial. Please listen to me with patience.'

Marston sat on the end of the bed and nodded agreement.

'Thank you. Beneath this house we have made a secret meeting place. There also is my communications room where I am able to keep in touch with fellow members in the Low Countries and in Luxembourg. I tell you this in confidence because I must convince you that La Promesse is to be taken seriously ... The question is this. I must ask you before the others arrive. What do you know about Paul Schengen? The man you were due to meet tonight in London? The man who is a photographic artist and writer living in Vianden, Luxembourg?'

'I have never met him, but was looking forward to doing so. But why do you ask? Why is he so important to you now?'

'I will tell you. La Promesse distrusts Schengen. I believe him to be a KGB agent actively engaged in recruiting susceptible men and women—particularly artistic and often unstable types. He flatters them with his attentions, invites them to his notorious Les Pins at Vianden, and then presumably decides whether they are suitable for further indoctrination … You do not need me to tell you more. By your writings we know that you have not only studied this problem but are aware of the dangers.'

'Did you know that Schengen was coming to London before you decided to abduct me?' Marston asked quietly.

'No sir, we did not. He is often away, and our representative in Les Pins cannot always know where he is going, but she is his housekeeper and can usually tell me when he will be away and what sort of party he is planning and when it will take place. The invitation card on your mantelpiece mentioning his name was a surprise to me.'

'Then why have you brought me here before I had a chance of meeting him in London?'

'Through our Louise in the château, we knew in advance that he would be away, and so we planned a meeting here this evening of a few of our people in Belgium and Luxembourg. Our man in Vianden, to whom Louise reports when she can, will be present and we want you to meet him and the others when you have agreed to help us. I could not postpone this meeting when we had already made our plans to have you with us, although I admit that if you had offered to take *me* to the party in London tonight I should have accepted, and somehow postponed our other plans … You will appreciate my dilemma, Mr Baines, but I assure you that I would rather have you here now as an honoured guest than have postponed your visit.'

'Very nicely explained, Schmidt, but if you will excuse me I should like to rest now. You have given me your confidence but I must consider your suggestion. If I decide there is no way in which I can co-operate, I presume that you will help me to get back to England at once?'

Schmidt smiled and went to the door.

'I do not think you will want to return until you have heard what our friend Philippe from Vianden has to say. If for no other reason, I am sure he will give you some facts which you will find valuable as a professional writer … Rest well, Mr Baines. Come down when you are ready. You are our guest, and the key to this door is on the inside.'

Marston made no answer to the last comment and lay back on the bed to think over what he had just heard. He was inclined to believe that Jan Schmidt was genuine. It was possible that La Promesse might well be more important than London assumed. It was still his duty to investigate this possibility. But did Schmidt know or suspect that he was a British agent? Did it really matter if he did, because La Promesse was certainly on the right side in their fight against the KGB. And there was something in Schmidt's clever assumption that he, Marston, must have some valuable experience for promoting the cause of freedom against the tyranny and subversion now stepping up its attack on the West. To help in this battle was still his duty and as he was now in Belgium with an admirable opportunity of finding out more about Schengen through La Promesse, he decided to stay and investigate Schmidt's activities as well. Later he could report to Peter Pendent on his secret telephone number.

Having reached this conclusion and decided to sleep for an hour or so he was suddenly disturbed by a commotion downstairs—a ringing bell, then a man's voice edged with hysteria and Madame Schmidt expostulating. Marston opened his door and stepped on to the landing from where he could see into the hall. The visitor was a balding, middle-aged man.

'But Madame, I must see your husband at once. I have grave news and have driven fast from Vianden.'

'Calm yourself, Philippe. We have an important visitor from England resting upstairs. Speak quietly. Jan is next door with Dr Carter. Wait here and I will telephone him.'

Marston also waited quietly on the landing while the visitor paced nervously up and down the hall. A few minutes later when Schmidt opened the front door Philippe rushed at him.

'Listen, Jan. This is urgent—before the others come. I saw Louise yesterday. She was greatly distressed and could not stay for more than a few minutes. She has proof that Schengen, if not actually organizing international demonstrations on May Day, has details of the plan and that tomorrow, Saturday, there is to be a black mass at Les Pins attended by those who will receive instructions. Four hours ago a woman's body was recovered from the river. I have seen it and identified Louise. I am sure they have murdered her and doubt if the police will take much action. I suspect Schengen's influence there.'

Marston stepped forward from the shadows, hesitated, and then went back to his room and slept for an hour. He was wakened by a knock on the door. It would be interesting to know whether Jan would tell him about the murdered woman. It would be suspicious if he did not, but when Jan came into the room he told Marston what his agent had reported.

'Yes, I heard him, Jan,' said Marston. 'I could hardly fail to do so. Tell me more. I have decided to help you if I can, but I must know more about La Promesse and how it works. You are right when you suggest that such facts would be useful to a writer. I may spend a few days over here and would certainly like to know more about the sinister Schengen. Rather intriguing to think that he is now in London with my publisher. What is he up to in his château at Vianden?'

'This is indeed good news. Thank you for your offer of help, Marston … I may call you Marston now, surely?'

'Oh yes. I am always on Christian name terms with my kidnappers. What do you want me to do?'

'We had hoped that you would attend our meeting later. Our aims are not secret, but it is as well that our members remain anonymous. Our enemies want to know who we are, and you have just heard that they do not stop at murder. I want you to see for yourself what sort of men and women are pledged to fight dictatorship in any form. We need advice on how to promote our views and aims to ordinary people. Will you speak to us tonight? And then if you have a few days to spare you might care to go out into the country and see how our friends are working in their areas.'

'Yes, I will stay tonight,' said Marston, 'but none of your members is to be told that I may visit them later. I shall make my own way and form my own opinions. You will supply me with an old car and enough Belgian francs for the needs of Marston Baines the writer engaged on research for a new book … And I should have a passport and a list of the names and addresses of a few of your people who will give me any information I require. Now tell me why you are so suspicious of Paul Schengen? He can hardly be a murderer if he is in London. Why do you believe he is a KGB agent?'

'I have told you that we suspect him but have no definite proof. Somehow or other the woman Louise who has been murdered has heard or seen something which suggests that Schengen is implicated in a plot for Marxist demonstrations on May Day, which is not many weeks ahead. In my opinion it is possible that somewhere in Les Pins, the hell-hole of this Schengen, there is hidden proof of his traitorous infamy. If the governments of the West could know in advance of the plans for May Day many lives could be saved … La Promesse wants those plans and now, my friend, this very minute I have the big idea … The really big idea … You, my dear Marston, are the man who could gain entry to Les Pins … Yes, you! You have been on the fact-finding trip, and because you could not get back to London for tonight's party, you pay Schengen a friendly call while you are in the enchanting Duchy of Luxembourg. The famous author calls to greet another author who shares the same publisher … Would it not be possible for you to suggest to Schengen that you might share some of his advanced views? It is you, Marston, who can most easily get into that house and see whether our suspicions are justified.'

Marston smiled to himself before turning to the eager Jan.

'Yes indeed, I might do that, but when I have left this house tomorrow you must make no attempt to contact me. I must be left alone. If there are enquiries from England you do not know where I am. If I want you, or the help of La Promesse, I will telephone you. I may, or may not, visit any of your members when I leave here but I shall listen to them with interest presently.'

5

Simon's Chance

The four young people returned to London on Sunday morning. As soon as Mrs Brown had retired to her cottage, after promising not to gossip in the village about Marston's disappearance, Simon had telephoned Peter Pendent on his private line. He reported Marston's disappearance and the possibility of an escape by helicopter, and played back the message on the tape-recorder.

'Shall I stay on here and check up on this chap in Eastbourne in the morning, sir? Might be difficult to get information on a Sunday but I could find out whether there really was a conference.'

'No. Get back here as soon as you can. Report by yourself and don't discuss the possibilities too much with your friends. Forbid them to mention Marston's disappearance to anybody ... Get a few hours' sleep else you'll wreck yourselves driving back.'

Simon told the others briefly of his orders. Kate and Rosina went up to Marston's bedroom for a few hours' rest while Simon and Charles dozed in the sitting-room. Dawn came too soon, but with the help of the girls they raided Marston's larder and enjoyed a good breakfast with excellent coffee.

Charles, as usual, did most of the talking.

'Simon has got to see his boss as soon as we can get him there. Incredible as it may seem, this man Pendent doesn't want the benefit of our advice. It might be years before Simon sees his beloved again, but she is coming home with us. It would be a good idea if they share the back seat while Kate takes the wheel and I give her helpful advice.'

And so it came about. The journey to London was easy and uneventful, and Simon was deposited on Pendent's doorstep in Mayfair well before noon.

'I'll be waiting to hear from you, darling,' whispered Rosina as she kissed him. 'Telephone me when you can and don't let him bully you. I'm anxious about Marston.'

So was Simon, but even more apprehensive about his interview with Peter who, on the telephone, had not been particularly concerned about his uncle. Perhaps he thought that Marston was capable of looking after himself? Or that he had planned to disappear in this way?

Elizabeth Pendent opened the door to his ring. 'He's in the upstairs study and waiting for you, Simon. Go straight in and I'll bring you some coffee.'

There was nothing of the fashionable West End publisher about Pendent this morning. The charming, talkative host of last night's party might never have existed. He had been replaced by a cool, tough-looking business executive sitting behind a desk in his private office. He nodded to a chair and Simon sat down feeling like a guilty schoolboy called to the headmaster's study.

'Any more news since you telephoned, Simon? You're sure that you've searched the cottage properly?'

'Everywhere except the attic under the roof. That is locked and my uncle once told me that he has the only key which never leaves his person. I have never seen inside it. Apart from this we have searched every room and the garage and his car. Everything is normal and I have brought his tape-recorder thinking that you might like to hear his message again.'

'Yes, we'll listen presently. Did you see Mrs Brown-next-door, before you left this morning?'

'No, sir. Her bedroom curtains were still across the window …
She won't talk about Marston. The village is used to him going away
suddenly, but she seems a little hurt because he always tells her when
he is going. And, as I told you last night there was a helicopter over
the village and I believe Marston has been kidnapped by the Belgian
who calls himself Schmidt …'

'Steady, Simon. Do you seriously believe that a man of Marston's
experience would allow himself to be tricked and kidnapped without
a struggle?'

'Yes sir, he might if he suspected this man and thought he would
learn something of value to us by going with him, or indeed if he
was on to an idea for a story. If he's alive and well we shall hear
from him, surely. Somehow he will get a message through. And
surely we can find out something about the helicopter and whether
the man who calls himself Schmidt really attended the conference
at Eastbourne.'

'Yes, we can do those things. The helicopter has already been
found deserted in a field near Felixstowe and the coast. I have no
doubt that there was somebody like Schmidt at Eastbourne. Now
tell me again *everything* that the four of you did and discovered from
the moment you left here last night. Everything. What you said on
the telephone is on my tape, but go through everything again and
we will listen to Marston's voice at the appropriate time … Give
me his recorder.'

Simon handed it over and began his story including the incident
of the police car which he had forgotten to mention on the
telephone. At this stage Elizabeth arrived with coffee and Peter
asked her to stay. Simon recalled how they had searched the garage
and the cottage and confirmed that Marston had been working at
his typewriter before he had been interrupted by his visitor.

'How do you know he wasn't expecting him—or her?' Elizabeth
interrupted quietly.

'Mrs Brown told us that a man in a "tweedy hat" had been asking in the village for Marston. It's possible that my uncle was expecting him. I hadn't considered that, but I do know that he is often visited by strangers who want to talk about his books, and he often uses his recorder to remind him of an eccentric character, or an incident that would help him with a plot ... The bit about dressing like a "typical English gentleman" is confirmed by Mrs Brown's reference to his hat, and Marston did hint that he *might* be disguised by wearing a wig as well ... May we have his message on again, sir? What he says suggests to me that the man was a character who might be credible in a story.'

Marston's voice came to them again. Simon pictured his slightly sardonic smile as he described Schmidt skilfully in so few words. Peter listened impassively and again Simon wondered what exactly was the working relationship between the two men?

'I'm convinced that this recording is exactly in keeping with Marston's methods, sir. I believe he's been tricked in some way and kidnapped. At the time he spoke these words in his recorder he cannot possibly have been suspicious of his visitor. Will you allow me to follow this up and try to find him?'

'No, Simon. I will not. Don't lose your sense of proportion. Marston is near retirement, but he still knows his way about. You can't seriously believe that he would allow himself to be kidnapped without a struggle. Forget him, because I've got an important assignment for you, and remember that Marston is still working for us and that I expect to hear from him ... Now listen carefully while I brief you for the most important job you have yet tackled for us—and the most important for your future.'

Simon realized that Elizabeth had left the room, and that he was being reprimanded. Peter got up and walked over to the window.

'I have just been telephoned by Schengen, who is now on his way back to Vianden. He has asked me that you should follow as soon as possible because he has material to show you for another book which, I have suggested, we might well be prepared to publish. You have made a very good job of *The Delectable Duchy*, Simon, and when I admitted that I could spare you for a week or so he was delighted. He told me that he had already invited you and your girl and that you would both be welcome at any time. You did your stuff well last night.

'It could be that he is more interested in your Rosina than in you. It will be your responsibility, not mine, if you take her, but why not ask your married friends? You've worked together before, and if they agree, you could go in two cars, and take a few days to get to Luxembourg. I told Schengen that you had some holiday due to you, but it's up to you whether you tell him that your friends are with you. They haven't been invited to Les Pins, but it wouldn't be a bad idea to have them in the background. The Duchy is a small place and there are several attractive towns and villages in the part of the Ardennes they call "Little Switzerland" on the German border, but of course you know about that because you've worked on the book. Go and talk to your girl and your friends. I can give you until tomorrow for your decision, but if Rosina does not want to go I shall understand. But you must go, and I shall notify Schengen myself.

'I have to know quickly the truth about this man and what he is up to. *This is your chance, Simon.* Perhaps your only chance to prove that you can function successfully without Marston. We must know what is going on in Les Pins. Schengen has asked for you, and that may mean that he thinks you are vulnerable. He may want to recruit you, and so unless you can prove otherwise, think of him as a clever and unscrupulous enemy of the West and our country in particular. We have unsubstantiated warnings and hints from our people across the Channel that we are close to a showdown. I distrust Schengen. I believe all this business of arty books and photographs is a blind. I want you to prove that my suspicions are well founded, and confirm that his house at Vianden is the headquarters of a dangerous organization ... See you early tomorrow and I'll give you further instructions then.'

6

The Pop Shop

A few days after Simon had received his instructions, the four young people arrived in Luxembourg City. Charles and Kate had been delighted with the idea of the trip, and Simon was relieved that Rosina would have their company while he was busy about his affairs. He had explained his situation, but told her frankly that he was not keen on her sleeping at Les Pins, although apparently she had been invited to do so. She had not taken kindly to this suggestion and had returned to the subject when they were on the last lap of the journey on the trunk road E40 from Brussels to Luxembourg.

'I hope I'm not supposed to be sleeping in a different hotel from you, Simon. May I know how many nights you are staying in the city, and why we're not going straight to Vianden? Perhaps arrangements for my disposal have been made by Peter Pendent, who obviously doesn't believe I'm capable of looking after myself?'

'Don't be bitchy, darling. Peter has suggested a hotel called La Petrusse and we're all staying there tonight. I'm sorry I can't tell you more, but I've got to report to another address in the city for instructions. You know I have to do this sort of thing. I love you, and now that you are here please don't make everything more difficult for me. Charles and Kate understand, and they like to have you with them … As for Les Pins, much depends on my orders, but I can't work as I should if I'm worried about you. It's my job to discover what Schengen is really doing, and I agree that nobody is more likely to help me than you. But we don't know anything much about his household. He's never mentioned a wife. We don't know what sort of an establishment he's running, and I'm not going to have you in Les Pins until I've found out more about it ... Ostensibly I'm going there to discuss a new book. When I meet him I shall explain that you are staying in the town with our two friends until we have finished our business talk and then we'll see what happens.'

'You're not convincing, Simon. You're old-fashioned and suggesting that I can't look after myself. In London, Paul told me that he had lots of parties of interesting young people. I can't come to any harm if it's like that ... And another thing. Charles and Kate are married and they don't want me all the time.'

Simon laughed. 'I don't mean all the time, love. It's true that I am old-fashioned about you, but please be patient until I know more about Schengen, and why he is so keen that I should come over at once to talk about this new book. He may want me for something else, and that something is what I have to find out ... He might have had his doubts about me if I had declined his invitation or refused to bring you ... There's a street map in the glove rack in front of you and we're in the outskirts of the city now. Please map-read me in. Peter marked the hotel with a cross. Charles is on my tail and he'll follow us.'

Rosina, still looking mutinous, did as she was told and ten minutes later the two cars drew up outside La Petrusse.

Three rooms had been reserved for them and after tea in the lounge Simon excused himself. 'Not sure when I shall be back. Don't wait dinner, but I'll telephone if I possibly can if I'm going to be late.'

Rosina did not look up as she said, 'Please don't put yourself out in any way for us, Simon,' and then as Kate looked at her with disapproval she added, 'All very well for you two, you're married,' and followed Simon into the reception hall. He had his back to her, studying a street map of the city on the wall. The girl behind the counter was polishing her nails and didn't even look up as Rosina put her hand in his.

'Sorry, darling. I was bitchy again. Forgive me. Come back soon as you can, and I won't ask any questions.'

Simon left her unhappily. He knew now why his superiors had occasionally hinted that life for him in the service of his country was sometimes going to be an unsupportable strain. Marston had never married. Peter and Elizabeth seemed to make it work, but that might be because they were administrative rather than on 'active service'. But why should Peter hint that the secret of Les Pins and Schengen might be Simon's last chance to prove his quality? He had not actually forbidden Rosina to come too, but said that the responsibility was his. It was clear enough that his superior had admitted the value of a party of four young people who Schengen had already met.

Simon's instructions were clear. He was to go as soon as he arrived to a house called the Pop Shop, and to ask the proprietor for a cassette of Marlene Dietrich singing "Where Have All The Flowers Gone?"

He remembered Peter's sardonic smile as he added, 'Almost before your time, Simon, but I'm glad today's younger generation admire the singer's artistry and the sentiments expressed. The man to whom you will ask this question will know who you are. Not likely that anybody else will ask him for that particular song, and as soon as you have been accepted you are under his orders. He is our representative in Luxembourg, and the situation at Vianden is his particular worry. You will report to him.'

And so Simon went out into the evening sunshine and the clean, bright streets of the most attractive city he had ever seen. He had memorized his route and although tempted to take a taxi to save time, he decided to walk and learn something of the layout of Luxembourg. His destination was in a small street near the railway station, and the map had indicated that the shortest way was to cross a huge bridge over a ravine which was now a magnificent public park.

He found the Pop Shop without much difficulty. The window was packed with portable radios, record players and cassettes and backed with coloured posters of pop stars. There was nobody in the shop but as he closed the door he heard the soft warning of a buzzer. Then a bright spot light was switched on and he was still blinking when a man sauntered into the shop through a door behind the counter.

Simon stepped out of the beam and spoke in French. 'Good evening. I was just passing and your window reminded me of a cassette that may now be rather out of date ... Have you a recording of Marlene Dietrich singing her famous "Where Have All The Flowers Gone?" I should prefer it sung in English.'

The man smiled, walked across to lock the shop door and pull down the blind. 'Yes,' he replied in English, 'I can oblige you, but we will talk in my office. My name is Jake and you are Simon Baines. I have been expecting you, but you have wasted no time. Follow me.'

Simon did so, feeling fairly sure that he was going to like this man's personality. Jake led him into an untidy but comfortable office. Racks fixed to the walls were packed with discs, cassettes and radio receivers. On the desk was a small closed-circuit television screen now showing the empty shop.

Jake smiled again as he sat down and pointed to another chair.

'Very useful and uncomplicated little marvel of science, Simon. I can inspect my customers before they can see me. The shop is now closed for the day and I usually enjoy a beer at this time. I hope you will join me and we can then get to know each other better.'

Simon nodded his thanks and watched his new boss carefully as he produced two glasses and cans of Stella from the bottom drawer of his desk. He was fair, slim, clean-shaven and handsome and wearing jeans and T-shirt under a denim jacket. Simon guessed his age to be on the right side of forty and that his women customers would find him irresistible. As he took his glass he realized that Jake's grey eyes were hard and keen.

'We'll take it that we've heard that the flowers have gone, Simon. I know that Pendent likes this cloak and dagger stuff, and he has described you to me. We've little time to spare, so I'm doing the talking and you the listening. Questions later. From now, until you get back to London, you are under my orders, and until the present problem is resolved there must be no communication with London except with reference to your work for the Pendent Press. I am responsible for the Duchy of Luxembourg and Belgium, and you are responsible to me and I will tell you later how we shall communicate. I shall want daily reports …

'Another important fact of life for you, Simon, is that you have brought your girl and two friends. I am told by London that all three have previously been involved in some of your uncle's cases and are trustworthy. I do not believe that any human being—particularly in our business—can be respected as trustworthy unless he or she has proved to be so under pressure … No, calm down. Don't say something you will regret. I've nothing against your girl or your friends—yet. But you must understand that whatever pressures are put on those three, I cannot promise to be responsible for them. The risk is yours, but I do appreciate that Schengen will be more likely to trust *you* because you have brought the girl and this young married couple. He obviously thinks he's going to get something out of you. He almost certainly wants to recruit you and he may have taken a fancy to your girl. It will be up to you both to decide how to deal with such a situation but as your friends will be staying in the Vianden hotel which I have arranged for you, there will always be a room there for your girl in a crisis … But it's up to you to play it your way … Schengen is not a nice man … Now for your questions and pass me your empty glass.'

'All that you have said is understood, sir—'

'Jake, if you please. I'm Jake to us all. Presumably Peter told you of our suspicions of Schengen?'

'I hope he told me all that he knows. He believes he is a KGB agent specially interested in recruiting young people to work in their own countries. I appreciate that this avant-garde act business at Les Pins is a very good cover for what he is really up to … But Jake, I want you to tell me more and what you expect of me. Peter will have told you that we have been deliberately cultivating Schengen and, from the business angle, we have been successful. He thinks Peter is a good publisher, and so he is. I think Schengen a clever artist and writer, but beneath all that there is something I *feel*, rather than something I know …'

'And what's that, Simon?'

'Old-fashioned word for it, Jake. I think he's evil. I know someone else who senses that sort of thing and is rarely wrong.'

'And who is that?'

'My uncle Marston. Did you know he's been kidnapped by a Belgian chap who somehow got him into a helicopter on the Downs near his cottage? I wanted to follow this up but Peter sent me here. He didn't seem particularly concerned about Marston. Have you any news of him?'

'I shouldn't worry too much about him, Simon. He was always rather a loner, I'm told, and I'm sure he can look after himself. Peter mentioned it, but Marston is on the last lap now and it's possible that Control has sent him off on some special mission. He may even have staged the helicopter. He's got a wonderful record, Simon, and he's a darned good writer, and that reminds me to tell you what I believe we are up against, and what you must do in Vianden.'

Simon shrugged. Only a few hours ago in the car Rosina had taunted him with a challenge that he was not worrying enough about Marston, but there was something odd about the way in which his superiors declined to discuss him.

Jake was now leaning back in his chair, fixing Simon with a cold, grey stare. As the younger met his gaze fearlessly he began to speak.

'I've only met you for a few minutes, Simon. I haven't given you a chance to say much, but I want you to know that I'm going to trust you and I believe we shall work well together. I believe, and hope, that you see the dangers facing Western civilization and our own country in particular. I do not know precisely what views Peter Pendent has expressed to you, but I can guess that as you served part of your apprenticeship with Marston that you share his views. I have never met your uncle, but I'm sure that he believes as I do—and you too probably—that the war we must win to survive is in the minds of people. Let us clear *our* minds on this issue. The KGB is working for the complete overthrow and takeover of the democratic West. *You*, Simon, are the sort of young man they would like to win now, and that is why you are going to Vianden.'

'You mean I'm to be a sort of guinea-pig? I share your views, Jake, but tell me now everything you know about Schengen and Les Pins. And are you suggesting that I shouldn't worry about Marston because he may also be on a similar, semi-private mission? I know he shares your views.'

'I wouldn't know, Simon and I've suggested that you shouldn't worry too much about him. And just one more word of caution. Do not discuss your mission more than you can help with your married friends or with your girl. I know the difficulties, and of course you trust them, but never forget that it is not prudent to share too much secret information. Try not to get too emotionally involved while you are on this job … OK? Good. While working on Schengen's book you've probably learnt more than I can tell you about this fascinating little country. The people are nice. Intelligent, friendly and hard working. Industrial in the south—steel. Most speak German and many English and French. Vianden, as you have seen from Schengen's photographs, is a picturesque little town on the German border on the river l'Our. The château is a sort of fairy-tale ruin—very large and crowning the wooded hill above the village. But of course you know this. Les Pins is on the hillside below and practically adjoins it. I shouldn't be surprised if there is some underground connection with the château. We believe—and you will help us to confirm—that the house under Schengen's direction is a centre of Soviet espionage and recruitment. In Victorian days I believe it would also be described as "a sink of iniquity". Only recently we have discovered that Schengen and some of his associates are practising black magic and Satanism. You may know what goes on under these dirty banners. Victims can often be photographed in compromising situations and then blackmailed. We believe that May Day this year will produce outbreaks of severe violence and anarchy in Western Europe—particularly in capital cities. We must get evidence and details of this plan and this is your charge. With evidence we shall take action before the end of the month. You have been given this responsibility because Schengen has invited you to Les Pins and obviously believes you are the type that he could use. He is vain and arrogant and consequently vulnerable. He may be suspicious of you, but I doubt it. You must go there tomorrow and try to contact me every day. The hotel at which your friends—and your girl if necessary—must stay in Vianden is the Hôtel de la Fôret. The proprietor is safe, and can be trusted in an emergency and you could use his telephone if necessary. If you can produce the evidence we want, we might get the police to raid the place. I will give you a gun for your own protection in the last resort. You are going into danger, Simon, but I am satisfied that you are the sort of person that Schengen might like to recruit for his work in Britain. Does he know that old Marston is your uncle?'

'Yes. I told you that he expected to meet him at Peter's party. He seemed very disappointed that Marston had not turned up. Peter told him that he had telephoned his apologies in the afternoon but that he'd had to go to see a friend in hospital. As you know, he's been abducted by helicopter, but Peter must be looking after that end. He's got a description of the chap he went off with.'

'Yes, of course, but we're not worrying about Marston. Not our job. No need for us to meet again until you've found your way around. Go straight to Vianden in the morning. Leave your friends at the hotel … Although your evidence is vital, play it cool. Incidentally, we believe that somebody at Les Pins has just murdered a woman who worked in the place. Her body was found in the river, but you may be able to give us more information. Good luck.'

'Thanks very much,' Simon said ironically. 'I shall need it.'

7

The House of the Pines

S imon found a taxi after his interview with Jake, and soon returned to the hotel. The others had waited for him, but the meal was not very lively because they deliberately refrained from questioning him. When they had finished, Charles announced that he was taking Kate for a stroll and then bent to kiss Rosina.

'Goodnight, love. Take care of Simon. He looks in need of protection ... As for you, Simon, you can give us your orders in the morning.'

When they were alone Rosina said, 'I've promised not to ask too many questions, but I want to know what I am expected to do in Vianden. Have you forgotten that I have also been invited by Schengen to stay at Les Pins? For the last hour you also seem to have forgotten that we are engaged ... Please take me out and explain yourself. I'm unhappy about us, Simon.'

He fetched her coat, took her hand and led her out into the moonlit streets and eventually to the great bridge spanning the ravine of La Petrusse after which their hotel was named. They stopped and looked down into the park below, and then he put his arm round her shoulders and held her close.

'I'm sorry, darling. Forgive me for being so surly but I am worried and there seems to be so much I cannot tell you.'

'Let me help you, Simon. Help in every way I can. I know that

I shall always try to do just that, but let me help you now by asking a few questions which should be easy to answer. Obviously you've had your instructions and I want to know how they concern me. I know it is your job to find out more about Schengen but you must realize that I am coming with you tomorrow to Les Pins. Is that clear? Surely you see that if you have to make excuses for me about staying in the house he will be suspicious? What is really worrying you? Can't you trust me to look after myself?'

'Of course I do, but what I have heard today makes me distrust Schengen more than ever. Until we know what sort of a welcome we are likely to get tomorrow, I agree that it is ridiculous for us not to go together. He knows we are engaged, and until we see how he is going to behave, and what really goes on in his house, we must assume that he accepts the situation … But darling, I am now sure that he is our enemy and a very evil man. What I have to do may be more difficult if you are also under his roof … just because I love you, and you are more precious to me than I can explain. But I do believe now, that together we must make an opportunity for him to give himself away and that, as you say, he might well be suspicious if you declined to accept his invitation to sleep under his roof. And even more suspicious if I made excuses for you. We shall certainly tell him that Charles and Kate are staying in the town and that we have all come for a holiday together.

'We should be in Vianden before lunch tomorrow. The couple running the hotel are on our side, and we can ask them to find a room for you if the situation at Les Pins gets too hot. Sorry if you thought I didn't want you there, but I've been told that I take you at *my* risk. Typical that they will welcome your help if it leads to results, but they won't take the responsibility if you're hurt, so you must see why I fuss a bit.'

'And I fuss about you too, Simon,' said Rosina. 'Let's meet trouble when we come to it and not before. The sooner we're out of Les

Pins the better, and when your job is done we'll settle down to enjoy ourselves. I wouldn't complain now if you found a café and we could just be together and forget your job. Promise that you won't say any more about Les Pins and Paul Schengen until we've got to Vianden ... Promise, darling?'

Simon promised and they had a happy evening and an easy, pleasant journey in sunshine the next morning. The two cars stopped for a coffee break in the fascinating little town of Echternach and it was here that Charles asked Simon what Kate and he were supposed to do while Rosina and he were at Les Pins.

'You can be honeymooners if you like! Vianden is a wonderful centre for walking or you could pass the time fishing. They catch trout in these rivers and as the Duchy is small you can explore it in your car. It's possible that you will be invited to some of Schengen's parties. We shall tell him that we've travelled together and that you're staying in Vianden, and we'll do all we can to keep in touch, but we must both be careful and cunning because the telephone in Les Pins may be tapped. I told you that La Fôret has been recommended to me and you know what that means. You *have* to stay there. The names of the proprietors are Jean and Marguerite Latour, but there is no need, at present, for you to indicate that you know that they are on our side ... But I hope, Kate, that you won't mind if I ask you both not to go too far away from the hotel for too long. Rosina and I will know more about the Les Pins set up in about forty-eight hours and there's no reason to suspect that we shan't be able to get out once we're in.'

'That's most reassuring for us all,' Kate said grimly. 'We are going to have fun, and thank you for the honeymoon idea. We'd never have thought of that without your help ... Wouldn't it be a better idea if Rosie stayed with us until you've reconnoitred?'

'No love, it wouldn't,' Rosina smiled. 'We must go together just to show the great Schengen that we're not suspicious of him, but

I am glad to know that you two are within reach. As Simon says, he'll probably ask you up to see his wonderful place. Let's go now. I've studied the map and we can't be much more than half an hour from Vianden. We'll lunch together at your hotel and then Simon and I will leave you to your honeymoon—you lucky people!'

And so they came to Vianden and soon realized why this part of the Duchy on the German border is called 'Little Switzerland'. The town was surrounded by towering, tree-clad hills on the highest of which they saw for the first time the mighty château which, from below, did not look like a ruin. Simon reminded them that part of these buildings were tenth and eleventh century, but most of what they could see was built four hundred years later.

'But where is, or are, Les Pins?' Charles asked.

'Schengen's book explains that it is hidden from the town by the pines, but it must be close to the castle walls … Our hotel called La Fôret is in the main street so let's make for that and eat together before we set off without you … I shall miss you, Charlieboy, and of course I always miss Kate,' said Simon.

Vianden's main street was narrow and ran downhill to the bridge across the river l'Our which, Simon explained, was dammed further upstream, where there was a powerful hydro-electric pumping installation.

'Schengen described and photographed his home town brilliantly in our book. I'm not surprised now by what I see. These little streets are mediaeval. Victor Hugo lived for some years in that house over there. Somewhere behind the buildings on each side of this main street there are sections of the old ramparts. Sort of fairytale place in a way—'

'Pity there seems to be a bad fairy or a wizard in the background,' Kate interrupted. 'Hurry and do your nasty job, Simon, so that the four of us can have a real holiday together … Let's go back now and inspect the honeymoon suite.'

The Hôtel de la Fôret was delightful. The proprietor was at the reception desk and when Simon introduced himself he fetched his wife Marguerite.

'Our best double room has been reserved for Mr and Mrs Hand by our mutual friend in the city,' Jean Latour explained. 'We have only a few other guests at present but other accommodation will always be available if required. You have only to ask either of us for anything which will make your stay in Vianden more comfortable. We like English guests here.'

So a nod was as good as a wink, and Rosina thanked him gravely and no more was said. Not even when they left the hotel as soon as they had lunched together. Kate tried unsuccessfully not to be emotional as she hugged Rosina and then turned to Simon.

'The four of us—and specially you two—must be going mad to be engaged in this sort of business ... Take care of her. Of course you will, but you promise to let us know if we can do anything.'

'Cross my heart,' Simon said as he closed the car door. 'Don't fuss and remember that you're on your honeymoon ... Cheerio, Charlieboy.'

The map showed them a lane leading to the château, and as soon as Simon turned into this they seemed to be in a different world. The pine trees were tall, and crowding densely onto the narrow road. They shut out all but a glimpse of the sky. No bird sang. No startled rabbit hopped across the road, and only the hum of the car's engine broke an eerie silence. Rosina's hands were clenched in her lap and Simon said nothing until they reached a small clearing with a track leading off to the right. He stopped the car and pointed to a post carrying a carved board with the notice—Les Pins—Privée. Then he unclipped his safety belt and put his arms round her.

'Relax, darling. This may be the last time we are alone together for some time. There's something else I must tell you before we get inside this place.'

She turned to him. 'Me too, Simon. It's too late now for you to persuade me not to come with you. I'm not going to desert you now, or any other time. What would you think of me if I suggested it? I know that you are scared for me about Schengen. No doubt you've been told more about him than you've told me—'

'That's true. I'm not afraid for you if Schengen turns out to be a womanizer. I know you will be more than a match for him, but I'm sure we're both going to be shocked—old-fashioned word I know, but I can't think of a better—by his lifestyle and certainly by his ideas. What I specially wanted to warn you about is that he is probably a Satanist and a practitioner of black magic. You know what this means? Remember what I told you about that business I was in with Marston and Patrick in Venice and Rome?'

'I'm not sure whether you told me the whole truth, but wasn't that when Patrick Cartwright first met Francesca and fell for her? … Tell me now. Does Schengen practise it?'

'Not sure, but I have to find out. Satanists often use their power to corrupt and blackmail their victims. The black mass which they practise in secret is a blasphemous travesty of the most solemn service of the Christian church. When I went to help Patrick in Italy that time, I saw part of one in the catacombs of Rome when I went in disguised with Marston to rescue Francesca's father. These people were prepared for a human sacrifice on their pagan altar of a girl who might have been Francesca, and whose father, from whom these devils were trying to get information, believed to be his own daughter. The man we met at Peter's in London, and who we shall meet again in a few minutes, is suspected of being a Satanist and he is the sort of man likely to be a leader of such a cult … You are very precious to me, my darling, and I am tempted not to obey my orders.'

When she raised her head from his shoulder to kiss him he saw that her face was wet with tears.

'But you won't turn back now, Simon. We will go in there and face that man together. I'm not so concerned with the wickedness of Schengen as I am with helping you. He must *not* be suspicious of either of us. You have got to do your stuff about the new book, and wait for him to give you the hint and the evidence you want. I believe he will enjoy plenty of flattery and we can both give him that. I don't think he'll chance making a pass at me when we're together, and nothing you say now will stop me from trying to help you. We must work together, but if I become too much of a responsibility by making everything too difficult for you I can, I suppose, go back to the honeymooners. After we're married it will be easier to make decisions like this … Tell me one more thing, darling, before we go in. You're worrying about Marston, aren't you? You're wondering why nobody else seems to be concerned if he has been kidnapped? Surely, if he's vanished of his own free will, it could be that he wants to put ideas into the heads of his enemies? I mean that he's vanished deliberately. Even to make the other side think he may be coming over to them.'

'Clever Rosie, as Kate would say. Could be as you say. I know nothing more than what we discovered at his cottage although I have been told not to fuss about him, but I'm sure something significant has happened. Anyway, if Paul Schengen asks about Marston we must play it very cool—just gone off on his own to work on a new plot. When the time comes for Marston to be sure that he's not capable of looking after himself, it's then that we shall have to worry. Thank you for what you said just now, and before we go on I might as well tell you that I'm glad you're here and going to stay with me. And another thing. I'm sure you're crazy to marry me.'

'I think so too. My mother tells me that I'm a wilful girl. But listen, Simon. I've just had an idea. My suitcase is in the boot with yours, but as we don't know exactly what is going to happen, let's not unpack—better still don't take the luggage out of the car, until we see what arrangements he's made for us. I don't mean that we'll run away, but I could pretend that I didn't expect to sleep in the house while you two are busy. This would give us the excuse to get back to the hotel and give you an opportunity to make a report which you certainly can't do from here. See what I mean? If he makes a fuss and protests that of course he is expecting me I'll butter him up and say how I've been looking forward to staying in his gorgeous Gothic home.'

'Yes, you are a clever girl,' Simon agreed. 'I would like a chance to report on first impressions before we get too involved. Now let's get it over. I know you hate too many trees.'

Neither of them spoke for the next few minutes. The private road through the forest was completely overshadowed. Simon remembered that once before Rosina had told him that she had never lost a childhood's fear of high winds and dense forests. When the road suddenly brought them into a semi-circular clearing he stopped the car in surprise. Their first impression of the exterior of Les Pins was that it looked like a Gothic prison. The house seemed to be built against the rock face above which was the summit of the mountain, and as the buildings were surrounded on the other three sides by a high wall, it was only possible to see a row of narrow windows on the top floor and the grey stone roofs above. But what they could see ahead of them was dwarfed by the majestic bulk of the château of Vianden thrusting its turrets, towers and ancient walls up into the April sky, and dwarfing the ugliness of the home of the notorious Paul Schengen, which had been built in its shadow.

Rosina's fingers were cold as she felt for Simon's hand. 'I hate it,' she whispered. 'The photographs in his book give no idea of how horrible it is … It's like a prison …'

As she spoke the big double doors in the wall ahead of them slowly opened automatically.

'So we are observed,' Simon said. 'This will not be the last of our surprises, darling … I didn't tell you before, but I have been given a small, but effective, gun …'

'And I'm not ashamed to confess that I'm thinking a prayer. Drive up to the front door as if we don't care a damn for all this showmanship.'

He drove through the double gates into a paved courtyard, and as he pulled up outside the front door he was not surprised to see the big gates closing silently behind them. Then the door was opened by one of the most extraordinary looking men he had ever seen. He was of medium height, thick-set, bald and clean-shaven. His pale complexion was emphasized because he was dressed entirely in black. His expression of blank indifference did not change as Simon opened the car door and got out.

'Good afternoon, sir. The master is expecting you. If I may have your keys I will bring in your bags and put the car away.'

'No, thank you,' Simon said as he opened Rosina's door. 'We would like to greet Mr Schengen first.'

Simon never forgot, nor ceased to admire Rosina's behaviour from that moment. She was superb in the way she acted the part of the slightly shy fiancée who did not want to show too much surprise in her new surroundings. This was not easy for either of them, because the interior of Les Pins was entirely different from the dim grey walls of the exterior. With one hand on Simon's arm and the other clutching her handbag, she barely glanced at the sinister manservant as he held the door open for them and then led the way into the hall. The interior lighting of Les Pins was their first surprise. The source of light was skilfully hidden but, as they soon learned, the entire house was always artificially lighted. Daylight had no meaning. Later they realized that windows of the rooms on the ground floor would be useless, because there was nothing to look at in the courtyard except the encircling walls. So there were no windows. Only bright, cold electric light reaching into every corner with a cruel, searching insistence, and illuminating pictures on the walls, which at first glance horrified Simon.

The corridor along which the manservant led them was carpeted, but as he paused and raised his hand to knock on a closed door it was opened suddenly from within by Paul Schengen.

The last time they had seen him he was dressed more or less conventionally in a velvet dinner jacket, but now he was wearing a robe-like, emerald green dressing gown with a gold sash. Rosina was wondering whether he should be wearing a jewelled turban as he seized her hand and raised it to his lips.

'My dear Miss Conway, this is indeed an honour and a pleasure. Welcome to Les Pins—and Simon, of course. I am delighted. Come in, my young friends. Peter Pendent telephoned that you were on your way. Thank you, Albert, that will be all, but please tell Maria that our guests have arrived and that we shall be glad to have her company in about ten minutes.'

This large room, which was luxuriously furnished, was not as brilliantly lit as the hall and corridors, but they both felt at once that it was not much used. Schengen offered what he called refreshment, and Simon explained that they had already lunched in Vianden with their two friends.

'You may not remember Mr and Mrs Hand at our party, sir, but when Peter gave me leave to come to you at once to discuss your new book, and to bring Miss Conway with me, it seemed a good idea to join up with them. They are as keen to explore the Duchy as we are, and are fascinated by your book. They will be company for Rosina while we are working.'

'Admirable idea, my boy. Admirable, and I hope we shall have the pleasure of seeing them here. They are at La Fôret, no doubt.'

He sat down on a sofa close to Rosina, who resisted the temptation to edge away.

'It will be good to have you young people here. We shall have a few more guests in this evening but we are always full at weekends and some very amusing and intelligent people arrive tomorrow. I feel sure you will both be stimulated by our entertainments and discussions … I must explain, my dear Rosina, that I am a widower. I lost my dear wife eight years ago when we were making this home together and I mourn her still. In a few minutes I shall introduce you to the charming Maria who is my secretary and hostess. I am sure you will get on together and she will do all that she can to make you comfortable and at home while I discuss business with your Simon, which I should like to do before our weekend guests begin to arrive tomorrow. Business before pleasure, I am sure you will agree.'

At first Rosina was uneasy. There was, as Simon had warned her, something nasty about Schengen. Even while making this rather pretentious speech she sensed that he was cold and calculating. He never looked at her but spoke over her head. Once she followed his eyes to an extremely unpleasant and suggestive painting on the wall, and was furious to feel herself blushing. But before she could answer there was a knock at the door and, at Schengen's call, a beautiful young woman came into the room. Maria—Rosina never knew her other names—was below medium height, slim, pale with black hair parted in the centre. Her eyes were large and dark and her lips scarlet. There was a Spanish look about her but she greeted them in perfect English as Simon stepped forward.

Rosina also stood up but Schengen did not move.

'These are our young friends, Maria. You already know what Simon has done for us on the first book, and you will soon know what he has to suggest for the next. Rosina is now in your care. Make her at home after you have shown her to her room. She must not be lonely at Les Pins. I have tried to explain that here, with us, many exciting experiences and surprises await our guests.'

Rosina feigned slight confusion.

'Thank you so very much, Mr Schengen—Paul, I mean. You are

most kind, but I didn't realize you wanted me to *stay* here. I thought you would be too busy with Simon. Of course I'm longing to explore your house and I shall enjoy seeing it with Maria but—'

'Nonsense, my dear. Of course you will be staying with my other weekend guests. Go off with Maria and you shall meet your young man again in an hour or so after we have had our first talk.'

So Rosina blew Simon a kiss, murmured a few words of thanks to Schengen and with a girlish smile followed Maria.

When the door had closed behind them Simon realized that Maria had barely spoken and that Rosina might even now be in some danger. And yet the Spanish girl had given a fleeting impression of defencelessness. How dependent, he wondered, was she on Schengen? And what sort of a staff had he here besides the sinister Albert?

But now Schengen had his hand on his arm. 'We will, if you please, continue our discussion in my study. Sometimes I call it my "Power House", I think you will appreciate it ... I congratulate you again, my dear boy, on your charming Rosina. I wonder how she could have imagined that we did not want her here? Of course we do, but we can leave her safely now with Maria ... I have some important matters to discuss with you.'

Simon was on his guard. In spite of Rosina's plan for getting back to Vianden later, he was not happy about the way in which Schengen had passed her over to Maria. There was nothing particularly suspicious about this attractive young woman except that she worked for Schengen, and everything about this man was suspect. Nevertheless, after only a few minutes with her, and only an exchange of formalities, he felt that she was under strain.

Schengen led him along some more brilliantly lit corridors and then down a dim flight of stone steps to a heavy door which opened at a touch of a finger on a hidden switch.

'I have spent much time and money on this workroom, Simon.

The book on which we worked together has shown how much I reverence the history of my country, but I also have a passion for the marvels of twentieth-century electronics … But that is not why you are here now. First I want to show you some more of my photographs, most of which are of the ruins of the château now above our heads. This room is one of many underground chambers cut out of the rock. Some were prisons and possibly torture chambers. Others were undoubtedly used for the practice of ancient mysteries—a subject of great interest to me and some of my friends. I am confident that you and Peter Pendent will soon appreciate the value of my research into these matters. There is much interest in these subjects amongst intelligent people today.'

He went on like this for several minutes and Simon, as a publisher, tactfully agreed with him. He knew that many people were fascinated by the occult. It was natural perhaps that his host should mention his interest so soon, but he was careful about the answers he gave to several subtle, probing questions on his own personal views. Simon had no doubt that every word of this conversation was being recorded on a secret tape, but Schengen might not suspect that his words were also preserved through a tiny microphone in his visitor's tie.

But Simon was now very uncomfortable. It was true that he had been warned by Jake that Schengen was not only a dangerous enemy but an evil man, and as Schengen began to show some of the pictures he had taken of the château, Simon became increasingly aware that this subterranean 'power house' was also an evil place. There were no windows, and the *shape* of the room was wrong. Ugly corners, a sloping ceiling of varying heights, a hideous carving of a goat's head on the wall just behind Schengen's chair. Indeed, wherever he looked Simon realized that there was nothing harmonious. No lovely curves, nothing to suggest the beauties of the natural world. No glimpse of sun or sky.

He remembered then that Marston, during a long walk on the Sussex Downs above his cottage, had once taught him the fundamental truths of the war in which they were engaged. He had stressed that there is always a war between good and evil, between freedom and slavery, between compassion and cruelty, and that in the twentieth century these issues are only too obvious. He had warned him also that the enemies of freedom are to be found amongst those carefully selected and trained men and women who set out to break down a nation's morale and destroy a people's will to resist. And so, with remembrance of these wise words of a brave and compassionate man, Simon found his courage again and made some practical suggestions about the book, and said how much he was looking forward to cooperating with him in its production.

'I'd like to take back some of these magnificent photographs to show Peter, sir. And if you have a rough synopsis ready perhaps we could discuss that now. I'm sure you are right about the special approach and appeal of the subject. I confess that it fascinates me personally.'

'I'm glad of that, Simon. I was always sure we should get on well together … Just one point. I shall be pleased if you will address me by my forename in future. I am Paul—not sir, to my friends. Now, it is time for us to drink together to the success of our new venture—and indeed to your future with the beautiful Rosina.'

Simon smiled his thanks. He remembered that it is always wise to avoid alcohol when on an important job so he made his excuses about drinking before sundown, and helped himself to a sealed bottle of tonic water from the bar which Paul had just opened up in the wall.

'Please yourself, my boy. Just relax for a few minutes because I want to talk to you about more personal matters, and may not have another chance during the next few days when the house will be full … You can speak to me in complete confidence. I have formed a very high opinion of your capabilities and knowledge of publishing. I know you can speak French and German and believe I can offer you a very much better job than you can get in Britain at the present time. Tell me more about our friend Peter Pendent. I'm sure he is a successful publisher but the business does not seem big enough for an ambitious young man like you. Sometimes I have wondered whether Peter has any other interests?'

Simon was able to deal with this sort of question in an ingenuous way, but while expressing his loyalty to Peter he confessed that he might have to make a change soon because he must improve his salary and safeguard his future.

'I'm not sure whether I told you, Paul, but Rosina has promised to marry me in the summer. Peter knows this, but you are right about Pendents being a small firm, and I don't think he will be altogether surprised if I make a move. May I ask whether there would be a chance of working for you? Are you interested in a publishing business of your own?'

'Very shrewd of you, Simon. Are you sure that it is still too early for me to add some vodka to your glass? Very well. I won't press you. Yes, I am considering my own publishing business and it will be unlike any publishing in Britain. You will soon see that I have many contacts with clever young artists and writers, all of whom despise the past with its shoddy old ideas and beliefs. They want to fashion a new society and a new world. They are weary of old moralities and are prepared to fight for new freedoms. I have a feeling you might be in sympathy with such people when you have met some.'

Simon hoped that he was not showing his excitement. He had not expected Schengen would show his hand so soon. He put down his empty glass and then took several steps round the hideous room.

'I'm grateful to you, Paul, for giving me your confidence. Of course I would like to better myself but you will understand that I must talk this over with Rosina. I presume that the job would be over here? And what do you mean by a "new society"?'

'It's a young world now, Simon. The young in heart have no time for old religions and moralities. If I may make a comparison, it is not the sort of world which your uncle, Marston Baines, believes in. Or seems to believe in. Where's he got to, by the way? I was curious enough to want to meet him at our party, but come to think of it there have been several peculiar rumours about him lately.'

Simon shrugged. 'Don't know much about him now. Haven't seen him for a long time. Why do you ask?'

'I've always admired him for his professional skill as a storyteller. I'd like to get him here for a visit one day.'

Simon was puzzled and a little apprehensive. It was possible—indeed probable—that the enemy was now aware of Marston's real job, but before he could reply a buzzer sounded on Paul's desk and he spoke into an intercom.

'Of course, Maria. You may bring Miss Conway down at once … Yes, Simon. You may tell your Rosina of our conversation. I should like to help you both, and I'm sure you can help me. Maria tells me that Rosina has a confession to make.'

One glance at her as she turned from thanking Maria for showing her the way, convinced Simon that she was not only excited but in very fine form.

'Oh, Mr Schengen. Please may I call you Paul? Thank you for everything. I've been such a fool and have come to apologize. I suppose I was shy or something, but I didn't realize I was expected to sleep here. I know you asked me to come with Simon and see your gorgeous home, but I thought that you both would be busy talking business and although you would be polite to me, I would be in the way. Now I've seen the lovely room you've got ready for me, I've come to say how sorry I am for leaving my luggage at the hotel in Vianden. Please may Simon take me back to fetch my case and explain to our friends? I'm so thrilled with this exciting place and I confess that I did pack my Luxembourg dress that you admired just in case we went dancing or something. I can't think how you thought of designing your office like this, and I think it's marvellous how you have transformed this old, ugly house into such a bright, colourful and exciting home of new ideas. I love new things and new ideas, and thank you for giving me the chance of sharing some of yours …'

She paused for breath, and as Paul was looking slightly dazed Simon went over to her.

'Of course I'll run you back, darling. I know the others will understand. Paul and I have had a splendid talk and I've got some exciting news for you. Thanks very much, Paul. We'll be back in half an hour.'

There wasn't much that Schengen could do except to suggest that Albert would go down to Vianden for her case if they would care to telephone first.

'Oh no, thank you. Everything is different now that I've seen this gorgeous place … We can find our way out, thank you, Paul. We know how busy you are.'

He let them go, but in the hall Albert was opening the front door to another visitor—a conventionally dressed young man with fair moustache and beard, who stopped on the threshold in surprise. After an appreciative glance at Rosina, he turned to Simon with outstretched hand.

'Hullo there! We've met before. I've got it—Simon Baines surely? Good to meet you here. Hope you're not leaving for good and will come back with your beautiful friend. I didn't realize you were one of us.'

'And who is that smoothie?' Rosina said as she got into their car.

Simon did not answer until they were through the double gates which opened for them. Then, 'His name is Timothy Hitchens. I knew him at Oxford and have met him once or twice at smart parties in London. He is a brilliant chap with a good job in the Foreign Office … Now, if you please, you will give me an explanation of the amazing performance by the rising young star named Rosina Conway. You know perfectly well that your luggage is still in the boot. What have you got to tell me? Something about the girl Maria, I guess.'

'Right again, darling. I just thought that you should tell your superior officer that Maria is absolutely terrified. So frightened that she gave me a hint that we should cut and run.'

'I see. All the more reason why we should go back. You really are my favourite girl, Rosie.'

8

Marston Again

On the same evening that Simon and Rosina discovered Les Pins, Marston Baines arrived at the Pop Shop in Luxembourg in an old saloon car with a Belgian registration. Marston did not like old cars, and as he had never been in this street before, his arrival was stately rather than dramatic. He was wearing the same old tweed suit in which he had been abducted, and before going into the shop he peered through the window to see if there were any customers within.

There were not. Nobody was there so he sat down thankfully and waited for attention. But not for long, and he did not even look up when the proprietor came in and switched on a light.

'I would like, if you please,' Marston said, 'a cassette of Marlene Dietrich singing "Where have all the Flowers gone".'

'She doesn't sing down here, Mr Baines.' Jake smiled as he came round the counter to shake hands. 'You are expected and I'm glad to see you. I live alone here and there is a bed available when you need it. Come upstairs. I have news for you.'

He locked the shop door and, as soon as they had settled in the comfortable living room above the shop, Marston spoke first.

'Not sure how much Peter Pendent has told you, but you should know that I have already reported to him and he asked me to get into touch with you. Did you know that I've been painlessly abducted from my Sussex home by a Belgian calling himself Jan Schmidt? He seems to be running the voluntary organization La Promesse.'

'Yes I know.' Jake smiled. 'We are aware of that lot. Earnest, rather disorganized, but not to be ignored, I feel. Difficult to believe that you were really fooled by friend Jan. I don't think Peter thinks so either. Could it possibly be that you thought it expedient to vanish for a while?'

'It could be, Jake. Not a bad idea to let the enemy suspect that I'm ready to come over to them … Could work the other way of course. I once wondered whether Jan was genuine. I'm sure he is. Are you?'

'Yes, but the organization wants watching. Maybe you can tell me more than I know? You've been visiting some of the branches since you left Brussels?'

Marston nodded. 'That's so. I'm impressed. They're not obviously trained for street warfare, but they have recruited some tough types, and they're single-minded about the enemy. Jan is particularly ill-disposed to Schengen and, subject to your approval, I think we might use La Promesse in a crisis, but much depends on news from Vianden. Peter told me that my nephew is on the job.'

'Yes, he is. I've seen him here and he should be at Les Pins with his girl by now. We've got a man and his wife called Latour running a hotel in Vianden and the couple your two brought with them are staying there. I understand that Schengen met them at Peter's party in London. Simon has got to report to me through the Latours who have the responsibility of getting a contact in the house. They're working on this now.'

'Schmidt has a man in Vianden, Jake. I've met him. He had a woman contact in Les Pins whose body has just been found in the river. She was on the domestic staff and the man is convinced she was murdered, because she had discovered something important. Did you know about the body in the river?'

'Yes, Latour reported that, but was not certain that the woman was employed at Les Pins. I'm expecting more news from him at any moment … But tell me more about Jan Schmidt. What does he really want from you? Or what does he pretend that he wants?'

'Says he needs my help in promoting the purpose of La Promesse. He professes to want an antidote to the continual stream of propaganda put out by agents of the KGB, and its acceptance by much of the media. He wants me to help him organize publicity for the other point of view. I mentioned this briefly to Peter, but obviously that's not for now. As I'm over here I'm at your service and it's up to you to decide whether we try to use the La Promesse crowd.'

'I'm not keen on too many amateurs getting in our way … I've got to be frank with you, Marston. Are you absolutely sure that Schmidt has no idea that you lead two lives? Why should he go to all this trouble with a helicopter when he could have tried you out in your own home? There was no need to dope and abduct you.'

'I did wonder whether he was putting on an act. He might even have been a KGB agent hired just to exterminate me. History has taught them that I've had a few successes. I'm on their first list of enemies to be exterminated. Of course I suspected Jan. He was being so obviously clumsy it seemed that he was worth investigating. I'm certain now that he doesn't suspect me and since I left Brussels I've visited, at his suggestion, three of what he calls his "branches" and met some of their members. I'm satisfied as to their aims and purpose, but of course they are only dedicated amateurs. But sometimes, just sometimes, zealots of this sort can be useful if only to distract attention from our own efforts. I am obviously interested in Jan's aversion to Schengen. He seems to sense that he is just the sort of man that the KGB would train and use for more recruiting. We think that too. You're in charge of this, Jake, and I'm here to help if I can. But it might be that La Promesse could be useful. It might be unwise to have two agents in Vianden both of whom want to see Schengen eliminated, but who don't know each other.'

'I get the point. It's possible that Schengen may have some influence in the local police, so for quick, rough action we might use La Promesse ... Peter, over in London, has given young Simon a tough assignment and I see the reason. He's worked with Schengen and he's got rather an endearing look of innocence about him. And the girl is a help, but I had to warn him we can't really be responsible for her ... Tell me, Marston. Shall I let Simon know through Latour in Vianden, that you're over here? I'm sure that he was anxious about you, but now that we've met and you've turned up here I see no reason to play you down. I had an idea that you really were coming in from the cold as some wise writer chap, like you, once said.'

Marston smiled. 'I'm not quite out and I'd like to work with you, Jake, but Simon must get a move on. If, as we believe, Schengen is the western European boss of the KGB now organizing revolutionary outbreaks in our capitals on May Day, there surely must be some written or taped records in Les Pins. We, and that means Simon, have to find them. It's not only proof that we need. We must take action to see that the plans don't go ahead. Maybe Peter is asking too much of him—and so are you—but you'd better put some pressure on.'

'Agreed. But I'll see that he knows we're both behind him. I'm not surprised that he doesn't believe you were really kidnapped and wonders where you are and what you're up to. Natural enough, really, as you prepared him for the sort of job he's doing now ... Come to think of it, I suppose there's no real reason why you should not pay a friendly visit to Les Pins? You missed the London party through an accident to one of your friends I hear. And knowing of your nephew's work for Schengen, who you were particularly keen to meet in London, you thought this a good opportunity of visiting the Duchy to get some background for your next story. See what I mean?'

'Only too well, Jake, but you must give Simon his chance.

Schengen is probably after him because he thinks he can use him. But he will certainly distrust me. In fact, if the KGB organization is as good as usual I'm almost certainly, as I told you, at the top of their list. I'm told that is the main reason why I'm booked for retirement. But let Simon know I'm about. You said just now that Schengen may have some influence on the local police? You mean bribing them to keep quiet? Or blackmailing somebody at the top?'

'Could be. We'll see whether they take any action over the dead woman. Maybe they'll say she just fell in or committed suicide. We're all agreed that Schengen has considerable powers and is not afraid to use them, but I'm not quite sure what you've got in mind about using La Promesse.'

'Listen, Jake. This is your show—not mine. I know I couldn't possibly influence you against your inclinations, but you might care to think this over. It is possible that we may have to take quick and violent action to get into Les Pins. You're not entirely confident about the local police but you may be able to get the soldiery at short notice. Maybe. I wouldn't know how that adds up in your territory … Jan Schmidt told me of the May Day rumours and he obviously believes them. He is well informed about Les Pins. He even suggested, as you did just now, that I pay Schengen a social visit. He has provided me with plenty of Belgian francs and the old Belgian car now in the street below.

'At the meeting of many of his members in Brussels which I attended I was to visit any of the branches. He suggested Arlon in Belgium and Ettelbruck away to the north from here and not so far from Vianden. Both these branches were lively. Jan had told them in Brussels that I was on their side about Schengen and the chap from Arlon informed me that he could always raise a gang of rough boys at short notice and take them anywhere I wanted. It is just possible, Jake, that we might care to take up this offer. I'm not sure how much Schmidt knows about me, but I am confident his organization knows as much about Schengen as we do and would do anything to get him eliminated. Don't underestimate Schmidt. The chap I spoke to in Arlon told me that he had at least twenty tough types who kept fit at weekends with long walks in your country here and have even explored the forests round Vianden. They could be quickly transported to Les Pins if needed. I was impressed by their zeal but we must remember that Schmidt and his bravos know nothing about you … But think it over. They might be useful.'

Before Jake could answer, a hidden buzzer behind a picture sounded a warning.

'Sorry, Marston. That's a signal that a message is coming through to my workshop downstairs. May be news from Vianden. Make yourself comfortable. Shan't be long.'

He was back in ten minutes and smiling grimly.

'Your Simon is doing well, and so is his girl who went to Les Pins with him early this afternoon. They have both been back to the hotel—ostensibly for the girl's luggage—and reported to Latour. Schengen is not wasting time. He has already tried to bribe Simon with an offer of work with him to start a publishing business and the girl—what's her name?'

'Rosina. A good one. Is she OK?'

'Yes. She's accepted Schengen's offer to sleep at Les Pins because she believes she can get some information from a frightened young woman who is apparently Schengen's secretary. I hope this girl is not working on Rosina. But the most interesting news is that the latest arrival at Les Pins is a young chap called Timothy Hitchens from our Foreign Office in London. Simon recognized him. Indeed they recognized each other. Come down to my communications room and we'll have a word with Pendent in London. Get him to check on Hitchens. I don't like the idea of bright young men from the F.O. being entertained by Schengen. It's at the weekends that he has his big parties and if May Day means what we think it does the next day or two may be a briefing party ... I agree that if we have to introduce an actual raid La Promesse might be useful. You could warn Schmidt without letting him know your official status, but let's sleep on that one and hope for more news from Simon tomorrow ... One other point. He reports that Schengen has a manservant who looks like a bodyguard and a potential murderer. I've left a message that we must have the May Day plans ... Now let's see what Pendent thinks. If he accepts the La Promesse plan you may want to get back to Brussels tonight to get Schmidt moving in case we need him ... Obviously you can sleep here if you like.'

'Thank you very much,' Marston said politely. 'I'm supposed to have retired.'

9

Beware of Timothy

Marguerite Latour, at the reception desk, expressed no surprise when Simon and Rosina arrived at the hotel.

'Alas,' she smiled at Rosina. 'Your friends have gone out to explore Vianden, and I do not know where you will find them … Perhaps Monsieur Baines wishes to speak with Jean? He is in his office over there. Please to go in, monsieur. I will see that you are not disturbed while Mademoiselle keeps me from the boredom.'

Simon entered the small office.

'So soon?' the hotelier smiled. 'You have done well if you already have something to report … Come upstairs. This room is only for hotel business.'

Simon was becoming familiar with 'communication rooms', but Latour's link with Luxembourg was no more than a telephone and short wave radio in a sparsely furnished office.

'Now tell me of your first impressions and what you have already learned of the unsavoury House of the Pines. Why are you back so soon? How did Schengen welcome you? How is your girl taking it?'

'If it wasn't for the intelligence and nerve of my girl, as you call her, we wouldn't be here now. More of how she managed it later, but it was essential for me to report at once because that place is like a prison. The gates to the courtyard are controlled automatically by Schengen's tough bodyguard. Obviously we dare not risk trying to telephone you unless we invent a simple code message. Every line out of that place is probably tapped.'

Latour nodded. 'We know the difficulties. You've managed to get out now and no doubt you'll do it again and that, I understand, is why you have been given this assignment. I am only the go-between and will help you if I can. But surely Schengen knows that your friends are staying here and dare not prevent contact between you? This is the strength of the present situation. We can perhaps arrange that if I do not have news from you every twenty-four hours we will get your friends to make enquiries from here. My responsibility is to report from Vianden to Luxembourg. I do not make decisions without authority. Now tell me what I am to report, apart from your safe arrival which I have already done.'

Simon realized that this man was his only link with Jake so he wasted no words.

'Schengen has already tried to bribe me with an offer to work with him here in starting a new publishing business and I have indicated that I am interested. He is working hard on me and I cannot be sure why. He stresses the importance of these weekends at Les Pins for what he calls the "young in heart". He makes no secret that he and his friends want to change society, and I have suggested cautious agreement, but I cannot make out why he is in such a hurry. So far, I don't think he suspects me, but it may well be that he does, and that I am in Les Pins because he wants to know more about my uncle Marston Baines, and might get at him through me. You will tell Jake that I am aware of the possibility. I have no firm evidence yet on the black magic front. He promises fun and games this weekend, but is not specific. On the wall above his desk, in the room in which he interviewed me, there is a head of a revolting goat. It is, I suppose, sculptured and then coloured. I remember that the goat is a symbol of ancient pagan religion. The man himself is intelligent, polished and urbane on the surface, but I suspect him to be ruthless and capable of any evil. His bodyguard is a manservant who looks like a thug and undoubtedly is one … Of more importance is the fact that a girl called Maria, who was introduced to me by Schengen as his secretary, and has given Rosina the impression that she is terrified, and even a hint that we shall be unwise if we go back to the house. I've only had a glimpse of this woman, who looks half-Spanish, but she seemed under considerable strain.'

Jean nodded. 'The body of a woman who we believe was on the household staff has just been found in the river near here. No obvious marks of violence, but we believe that Schengen has some hold over the local police and that nothing more will be heard about the matter … You will of course warn Miss Conway about Maria. She may be just trying to get information. It's an old trick.'

'We are both aware of that,' Simon snapped. 'I have another more important matter for you to report. Schengen tells me that the first weekend guests arrive tonight and more come tomorrow. As we were leaving just now a man arrived, who I know vaguely. He remembered me but was obviously surprised to see me and Rosina at Les Pins. His name is Timothy Hitchens and I first knew him at Oxford, although he is considerably older than I am. I have since met him in London. He is a very personable bachelor, and I was told he has a good job in the Foreign Office. Mention this, please, and I want London to investigate and to let me know as soon as possible. Now we must get back. If you don't hear from me in forty-eight hours you must assume that we can't get out of the place, so you must investigate. Mr and Mrs Hand will cooperate without asking questions. They've helped us before, and under the circumstances there's no reason why they shouldn't pay us a social call.'

Rosina was waiting and asked no questions until Simon stopped the car when they reached the turning to Les Pins under the dark pine trees. Then,

'Now tell me what to do about Maria and about that man we met as we were coming out. I'm sure I'm right about Maria. She really is scared but isn't sure about us. She knows about you because she is Schengen's secretary—and possibly more than that—but I have the feeling, or you can call it feminine intuition, that she wants to tell more and that is because, as she said, we are not like the others … Didn't that man Timothy say, "Didn't know you were one of us?"'

'Yes, he did. I'll look after Timothy and leave Maria to you. She's scared because a young woman who was on the household staff has been found drowned in the river. Obviously somebody pushed her there, and Maria is wondering whether she'll be the next … Now listen, darling. I hate involving you in all this, but I'm thankful you're here. You put up a wonderful show with Paul and if you go on acting your star part it will help me to be the ambitious and youthful publisher who is longing to get married to the most wonderful girl in the world, who is impressed by the skill and personality of his new employer … But, I must tell you now, that in my other occupation, we are warned *always* to be suspicious of any man or woman on the other side who suggests that they are getting browned off and asks for help to defect. That is when we may give ourselves away, and present the intended defector with information that he wants. I hate to mention it again but this is a world of double cross … You may be right about Maria but today I must leave her to you. If Schengen has a party tonight, she may be there acting as hostess, but be careful not to have any conversation with her in any of the bedrooms—particularly yours. I expect that they are all bugged and that conversations can be overheard or recorded on tape. Maria probably knows this, but you must be sure that she isn't tempting *you* to talk out of turn and betray us. She may well ask you in a girlish way for information about me.'

'In that case I shall give her girlish answers about my love life … Don't worry about that, Simon. I believe Schengen has some sort of hold over her. We talked in her little office and surely that couldn't be bugged?'

'Could be. She can't spend every hour of her life there. She may be terrified because she has discovered a secret—perhaps the same as the murdered woman—and wants to escape before Schengen realizes that she knows. And don't forget that if you talk too freely in her office, she may be recording you on one of those machines like Marston's. I know this is a messy business but we have to take some risks. Whoever we meet tonight, play up Pendent Press and the new book I'm working on with Paul. And beware of Timothy Hitchens. I'm sure there's something else I ought to be remembering about him, but I'll tackle him and leave Maria to you—but softly, softly …'

'I'll be careful, Simon. Of course Maria might try to get sympathy from you. She's rather attractive and, after all, you have the famous book in common. You both worked on it in your different ways. Let's go in now and get it over. Don't fuss about me.'

The big gates were open as they approached and several cars were now parked at the side of the house. As Simon pulled up, the front door was opened by the saturnine Albert.

'Allow me to take your bags now, sir. Miss Conway knows her room and you are on the floor below next to Mr Hitchens. The master refers to these two rooms as the bachelors' retreat, and I am to tell you that we dine informally at nine this evening, but he hopes to welcome you both in the Grand Salon to meet his other guests at half past seven … Now, if you will permit me, I will lead the way.'

The upper floors were a maze of corridors, steps and narrow turns and, like the rest of the house were brightly lit even in daytime. The doors of most of the rooms displayed a typed card with the forename or names of the occupants. Simon, who was trying to memorize the route from the hall, noticed that most of the rooms were for couples, but a few were labelled 'Privée'. The corridors and stairs were carpeted. Their footsteps were muffled and Albert had nothing more to say until he stopped outside the door labelled 'Rosina'.

'I trust you will be comfortable, miss. Please use the telephone should you require anything. It is Monsieur Schengen's pleasure to provide service for his guests.'

He opened the door and took in her luggage and Simon followed. The room was comfortably furnished, but there were no windows and they could hear the gentle hum of an air conditioner. Simon was relieved that there were no pictures on the walls.

'Thank you, Albert,' Rosina said. 'I'm sure I shall be comfortable, but will you show me Mr Baines' room. I should like to know where he is because without his help I might never find my way down to the salon. And I'm curious to see the bachelors' retreat.'

Albert merely inclined his head and led the way along the corridor and down a few steps into a short passage in which there were two doors marked 'Simon' and 'Timothy' respectively. Simon took his suitcase and, 'That will be all, thank you, Albert,' he said.

Just for a second the man's face showed a flicker of emotion, then he turned on his heel. At the top of the three stairs he paused to look back at them and then disappeared down the corridor.

Then Simon opened his door and drew Rosina into the room. In the gloom of yet another windowless room, she came close to him and raised her lips for his kiss.

'I'm no use to you, Simon,' she whispered. 'I'm scared of that awful man. He doesn't look human. Switch on the light and close the door ... Yes, like mine, there's a key and no bolt.'

He held her close and whispered, 'We may be watched now. Everything we say may be recorded on tape. I'm going to search this room when you've gone, but if we're going to fool Schengen we must pretend to be what he thinks we are. We have no reason to be suspicious of this place. It's true that we are surprised by what we see, but we must persuade him that we both want to get this job. We're guests of an artistic and remarkable man who is certainly wealthy and hospitable. This is a private house and not a hotel where the guests always lock their doors. Just play the girlish Rosina and I'll play the ambitious young man anxious to marry her as soon as possible. Nothing is more important to us both than this new job.'

He felt her relax and as he switched on the light the telephone on his bed table buzzed.

'Back to your room, darling,' he whispered. 'Lock your door and don't open it until I call for you and knock three times. If I'm not with you in forty minutes ring me on the telephone. No reason why you shouldn't ...'

She nodded and closed the door softly behind her as Simon lifted the receiver.

'That you, Simon old boy? Timothy here. Paul told me that we're neighbours and I've been looking for you about the place. I'd like to have a chat with you before we go down and meet the company. I gather that this is your first visit. Mind if I come in now—if you're alone?'

'Of course I'm alone, but I'm unpacking and changing ... Anything special? I mean, we shall meet downstairs, shan't we?'

'Oh, yes. It's just that as we're among a very few Britishers here I thought you might like to know more about this set up. Don't misunderstand me. I'm here with a girl friend too, and I thought that maybe the four of us could get together later.'

'No reason why we shouldn't,' Simon agreed. 'Give me about half an hour and then come along.'

He replaced the receiver thoughtfully. He had intended to search his room for a hidden microphone or even a camera, but now realized that by doing so before trying to get something out of Timothy, he might give himself away. Until he knew for certain that Timothy was suspected in London, it might be better to allow a conversation with him to be overheard and to see that he did most of the talking. Even if this room was bugged, it was unlikely that his own whispered conversation with Rosina just inside the door could have been overheard. And Timothy's reference to a girl friend was interesting. He had certainly arrived alone. Simon wondered if her room was next to Rosina's.

As he unpacked, bathed and changed he was, however, thinking more of Rosina and wondering how he could protect her from the contamination of what was going on in this house. And it was true that he was worried about Marston's curious disappearance and the fact that his colleagues were apparently unconcerned. But perhaps he was up to something on his own?

Then a knock on his door reminded him that he also had an important job to do, and that Peter Pendent had indicated that the solving of the secret of Les Pins was his big chance. And, as he called 'Come in' to Timothy Hitchens, he wondered whether this man's appearance here was really a coincidence?

Timothy, now resplendent in a cherry-coloured velvet dinner jacket and large bow tie to match, stepped forward with outstretched hand.

'Extraordinary meeting you here, Simon. Delighted to see you. Had no idea that you knew the fantastic Paul Schengen. As a matter of fact, one never knows who one is going to meet at these weekend parties—or indeed how many surprises Paul will have for his guests … Have you known him long?'

Simon explained the situation, that he was really here on publishing business but had not met Paul personally until the launching party for *The Delectable Duchy* in London a few days ago.

'You'd forgotten that I'm Peter Pendent's editor and have worked on Paul's new book for months. I'm here now to discuss another book, and he was good enough to invite Rosina Conway as well. She's going to marry me in a few months. Now tell me why you're here, and why you asked me if I was "one of us"? What's going on here? You're still in a nice, safe cushy job at the F.O., aren't you? Where does Paul Schengen fit in?'

'Too long a story to tell you now, old boy. Paul likes collecting interesting, original people. Some would call him a bit of a rebel, but that depends on whether you're old-fashioned, I suppose.'

'That's why you're surprised to see me here,' Simon smiled. 'I admit I'm old-fashioned enough to be slightly shocked by this place—and by the decorations on the walls. How did you first meet him? Your job is so very respectable, isn't it? Shouldn't have thought a chap like you would have had much in common with the artistic, progressive Paul Schengen. You must not be offended, Timothy. You didn't expect to meet me here and I'm surprised to see you … Maybe you share some other interests with him?'

Timothy didn't like this question and Simon realized that he was on the defensive. What is more he looked pale and ill, and his fingers were shaking when he unclasped his hands. Drugs perhaps? Or was he being blackmailed by Schengen in exchange for information from the Foreign Office? Or, was Timothy being used to spy on Simon Baines just because it was well known that Marston was his uncle? And, at this stage of Marston's career, his double life might be no secret to some of his enemies. The fact that this was now possible was the chief reason for his early retirement.

Simon sat on the end of his bed and smiled at his companion.

'Never mind, Timothy. You don't have to tell me your secrets. I shall soon form my own opinion of this set up and be back again in London in a few days. I'm here as a publisher and couldn't have declined the invitation even if I'd wanted to. And it was natural enough for Schengen to ask my girl as well. Tell me about yours?'

'Kathie will be here for the party. She's got a marvellous job in Brussels. Doesn't take her long to drive here … What's happened to that interesting uncle of yours, Simon? The writer chap. Thrillers isn't it? Haven't heard much of him lately.'

'Maybe you don't read the sort of books he writes, Timothy? Marston is still about and is published by Peter Pendent. That's how

I got my present job. He's still living down in Sussex.'

At that moment the telephone buzzed and he remembered Rosina.

'I'm expecting this call so you must excuse me, Tim. See you later,' and before he could complain, the representative of Britain's Foreign Office found himself in the corridor.

Simon lifted the receiver, but the caller was Paul.

'Ah, Simon! I'm glad to have caught you. If you and Rosina are ready, I hope you will join me for a quiet drink before my other guests arrive. You are strangers to Les Pins, and I would like to tell you something about the people you will meet later. I am anxious for you both to feel at home here—particularly as I hope our more personal relationship is only just beginning ... Albert will be waiting for you.'

This was as good as an order, so as Simon was leaving nothing incriminating in his room he did not even trouble to lock his door. Important for him to play the part of the innocent young guest. As arranged, he tapped on Rosina's door and she opened it at once.

'I was just going to telephone,' she whispered. 'You've been ages. Nothing has happened except that I feel very lonely. I can't forget that somebody might be watching and listening to us even now. I'm dreading this party, but I've put on the Luxembourg dress in the hope that he'll be flattered. Will I do?'

He reassured her in a normal voice and told her of Schengen's invitation. 'We'd better not keep him waiting, darling. Decent of him to ask us, as this is our first visit. You look gorgeous.'

He opened the door and heard her frightened gasp of surprise. Albert was standing on the threshold and for a few seconds stared at them without speaking. Then, in his toneless voice he said, 'I am to conduct you to the master. Please to follow me.'

Simon, with Rosina's fingers gripping his arm, wondered where the man had been hiding when he had knocked on her door, and whether he had overheard their brief conversation. He could not have been far away.

When they compared notes later, they were uncertain about Schengen's purpose in having them along in the hideous room where he had interviewed Simon earlier. Rosina maintained that he was trying to impress her with his worldly charm, but Simon believed that he was trying to warn them not to be too shocked by the other guests. Indeed, it was during this extraordinary evening that he first formed the opinion that Schengen's main interest in him might well be Marston. Little doubt that his uncle's enemies would be glad to have him in their power. It was also significant that he had asked one or two searching questions about Peter Pendent, but Simon did not share these doubts with Rosina.

At first Paul was at his most gracious. He had abandoned his strange robe and was now wearing an orthodox black dinner jacket with an orchid in the buttonhole. He congratulated Rosina and thanked her for wearing the Luxembourg dress. 'I wanted to assure you both, before joining the others that I am delighted that Simon is going to join forces with me. Honoured also that these new responsibilities will enable you to make your first home together in this beautiful little country. Many of my friends are aware of my publishing ambitions and I shall be happy to introduce you to them. It is important for you to understand that Luxembourg is not like London. It is more than European. It is, in a small way, international and my work and interest here at Les Pins is to make my home not only the most advanced centre for the arts in Western Europe, but a meeting place for all who believe in progress.'

There was more of this, with Simon nodding agreement when possible and Rosina thanking him and then declining another glass of champagne.

'We are here to learn how to help you and work with you, Paul,' she said. 'You seem to be telling us that we shall soon be among the sort of artistic and intellectual people who we should have no chance of meeting in London. Don't worry. We shan't let you down. Both of us know that you are giving us a wonderful opportunity of starting our lives together—far, far better than we should get in England.'

From that moment she abandoned her act of girlish surprise and excitement and Schengen was impressed.

'That is so, my dear. Do not be too bewildered or shocked by what you see and hear this weekend. I know all these people and have a good reason for asking them. Simon is going to help me make money out of them ... Now let us go into the salon where, no doubt, Maria has been busy preparing for our guests.'

The big room, which they had seen only briefly when they first arrived now looked very different. A long, well-loaded buffet table was against one wall and some of the furniture had been removed to give more space. Simon realized at once that the lighting now was more subdued with shaded lamps on some of the small tables. Maria, looking pale but beautiful in a long, scarlet dress was speaking to two white-jacketed waiters, and this reminded him that these two were the only servants he had seen at Les Pins. Neither Albert nor Maria could be so described, and yet somebody must keep the place clean and look after the bedrooms.

Maria came over as they stood just inside the door. Her eyes widened with surprised when she realized what Rosina was wearing, but she spoke directly to Schengen.

'We're ready now, Paul ... As you suggested, there are enough tables for the twenty-five guests and the men will bring in the cold food on trolleys at ten o'clock. There's plenty of champagne.'

Schengen nodded and led them over to the bar.

'Join us now, Maria. You will soon be too busy ... By the way, Simon, I was interested to hear that you know Timothy Hitchens.'

'Yes, Paul. I've met him in London but was surprised to see him here. I don't know him well.'

Then Albert opened the door and announced the first guests. Schengen went over to greet them and Maria, as his hostess, followed. This was the beginning of the most amazing party Simon and Rosina had ever experienced.

As both of them were modern language graduates they surprised some of those to whom they were introduced by replying in their own language. Most were European, but there were two powerfully built black African men, and a swarthy, surly, handsome younger man with a beautiful girl who had little to say, but who Simon judged to come from the Middle East. Another attractive girl complimented Rosina on her Italian, but a well-groomed French woman, wearing a short skirt and black boots, looked them up and down disdainfully and then turned her back. Schengen, who was certainly a good host, did what he could by introducing them as 'my gifted young editor from London who is to work with me here for a few days on a new book, and his charming fiancée', but it was not long before they sensed a very unpleasant atmosphere in the room. True that Simon had been warned, but he was soon aware that all these people were sharing something besides their political beliefs and activities. He knew about these, but as the drinks began to circulate, he realized that Rosina in particular was being watched with a sort of greedy anticipation. With horror then, he remembered the black mass he had witnessed in the catacombs of Rome, and knew that these people were Satanists. He took Rosina's cold hand and led her to a table away from the crowd round the bar. As they sat down Timothy and his companion came into the room. The girl friend was a tall, commanding figure, informally dressed in jeans and a tight black sweater.

'Sorry I'm late, Paul,' she called across the room. 'Business in Brussels kept me. I'll be telling you later.'

Several of the guests spoke to her as she pressed forward with Timothy looking rather foolish tagging along behind. Simon watched them speak to Schengen, and was telling Rosina about Timothy and their bedroom conversation when she said quietly, 'He's just seen us. He's telling Schengen who, I bet, is telling him to come over. Don't trust him, darling, or the ghastly woman with him. She's the boss of those two and I'll tell you something else important after we've got her talking.'

He wondered what he had missed, but was becoming increasingly impressed by Rosina's sharp perception and intuition.

'This is Kathie,' Timothy said as he put down two glasses of wine and pulled up two chairs. 'My old friend Simon Baines and—'

'Rosina,' she said as she smiled at them both. 'Thank you for joining us. We're a little bewildered by this grand party because we don't really know anybody. Did we hear you say that you work in Brussels, Kathie? What fun. What do you do?'

Kathie took a long drink and gave Rosina an even longer stare before she answered: 'Being new you wouldn't know that nobody at these shows would ask such a question. I know you two are English and that's enough for me.'

Timothy tried to cover up such rudeness, but Simon realized that they had both already been drinking too much.

At that moment Maria came up and broke an awkward silence by asking if they were enjoying themselves and was there anything they wanted? Kathie asked to have her glass filled. 'Sure and it would be better if you brought a full bottle.' Then suddenly Simon knew what Rosina meant. Kathie's accent was Irish and she hated the British.

'I'll find a waiter,' he said and pulled out a chair for Maria to sit down. She gave him a grateful glance and he noted again how ill she looked.

Timothy followed him to the buffet. 'Sorry about that, old boy. 'Fraid Kathie isn't quite herself. Working too hard I reckon, and said something about being held up on the autobahn because of an accident … Paul asked us to hang around you and Rosina, so that you don't feel out of it. That chap over there with a red beard is an artist—the one talking to the French bit in the black boots. She's something to do with newspapers and you might like to meet them. Tell me, Simon. How have you got involved with this mob?'

'Was going to ask you exactly the same question, Tim. You know why I'm here. I want a better job so that I can marry my girl and live more comfortably than in England. I shall have more responsibility and more chances working with Paul than I can in London. What about you? You don't quite fit in either. Maybe Paul has something you can't do without?'

They were at the buffet now and Timothy dropped the empty glass he was carrying. 'Yes,' he whispered. 'Maybe he has. How did you know? We'll talk again. Later, most of us will be going into the gambling room. There's roulette and almost anything else. Maybe we can help each other? You might want to know more about this outfit than meets the eye? Kathie is coming over for her bottle …
See you.'

Simon was very thoughtful as he struggled through the noisy crowd back to the table where he had left Rosina. On the way Paul, now with Red Beard and Black Boots, waved a greeting to which he replied, but he was still wondering about Timothy and how much he knew about Schengen's plans for May Day as he sat down between Rosina and Maria.

'Listen to me carefully,' the Spanish girl whispered. 'I must not stay with you much longer but show no surprise at what I say. Watch Paul over my shoulder, Rosina, and if he seems particularly interested in us get up at once … I know you two are different … No. Don't interrupt me. Listen. I beg you to help me. I am in great danger and must get away from this place. There has been a murder here and there may be another. I have a secret which is too terrible for me to bear alone and I must trust you to help me to escape with it … Somehow I will meet you later tonight. Albert is in charge when they are in the gambling room and that time will be best. I will let Rosina know when we can meet in my room. I beg you not to discuss this together until we can all meet later. Trust me and pray for me.'

10

Maria's Secret

Simon and Rosina did their best to mix with the other guests after Maria's dramatic disclosure. Both made special efforts to be agreeable and although Paul missed no opportunity of stressing his appreciation of Simon's work on the book, few seemed interested. Redbeard, who had been eyeing Rosina with appreciation, came over and introduced himself. 'My name is Dirck and I am the most famous artist in Amsterdam. My work is so advanced that few can understand it. Paul tells me that you are British. You are beautiful in a quaint, old-fashioned way and I would like to paint you—but not in that ridiculous garment. Come to see me in Amsterdam and tell me now why you are here?'

'Because I was invited by our host,' she replied. 'Were you invited too? I wonder why, if nobody can understand your work. May I introduce my fiancé?'

Redbeard shook his head and wandered away, but Simon noticed that several times during the next few hours he was watching them both keenly. Soon after midnight Paul announced that the 'Games Room' was ready for all who enjoyed a gamble. Albert led the way and then took charge of the proceedings and acted as croupier at the roulette table which was well patronized. Simon had played before and Paul instructed Rosina who won a little and soon lost more. Baccarat was also available but soon a few of the couples drifted away and then Rosina took the opportunity to make their excuses to Paul and to thank him for such a wonderful party. Simon added his thanks: 'And I'll look forward to more discussions about our future plans tomorrow, Paul. We're both too excited and tired to play any more now.'

'I'm glad you're both here and have enjoyed yourselves,' Schengen said. 'Remember that I've a lot to offer those who can dedicate themselves to my work.'

Nobody noticed them as they left.

'I suppose Maria knew where we were?' Rosina whispered. 'We must help her, Simon. Surely you can see that she's desperate? You believe she was telling the truth, don't you? She said "Trust me and pray for me". I trust her. Do you?'

'I'd like to, but we must get the truth from her tonight. I still can't be sure why Paul has got us here. I know why I've been sent, but be cautious of Maria. She may be so much in Paul's power that she's been ordered to find out more about us. And that might be something to do with Marston.'

The salon was in semi-darkness and smelt of stale tobacco and wine. The waiters had cleared away the buffet, and the silence was broken by the drunken snoring of a couple on a sofa. Maria was standing in the shadows near the other door. When she saw them she raised a finger to her lips and then beckoned to them. They followed her in silence until she had unlocked the door of her office.

'Thank you for coming,' she whispered. 'I thought it wiser to wait for you. I did not think you would be long in the gambling place … We must be quick. This is my small office where I do my typing. Here is my kitchen and sitting-room and through here is my bedroom where we shall be safer. We cannot be heard from the corridor and we shall hear if my office door is opened. Every door in Les Pins except the private rooms of Paul and Albert can be unlocked from outside with a master key.'

'Can we be overheard by microphones?' Simon asked.

'The guest rooms have them, I believe. Please do not interrupt me now with questions. I trust you both, although I do not really know you. I *must* trust you because you only can help me to escape from this horrible house. I must get out tonight or tomorrow. I have no car, but even if I had I am sure that Albert, who controls the big gates with a switch in the hall, would never let me out and I dare not ask the kitchen staff for help.'

Simon interrupted her.

'All that you say may be true, Maria, but if you want our help you must tell us at once why you are in such danger. And why ask *us*? We are new here.'

'That is why,' she whispered, and covered her face with her hands. 'Because you are not like the others. You do not, cannot know, how evil it is. The longer you stay here the harder it will be for you to escape … Cannot I make you understand that I *know* my life is in danger.'

Rosina, sitting next to her on the bed, took her hands.

'I trust you, Maria. Tell us why you are in danger and why you cannot leave here. This is not a prison, surely.'

'Very nearly it is. There are no servants here, only slaves. I am afraid because my friend has been murdered. She has discovered Schengen's secret and shared it with me. There may be no escape for you if they suspect I have told you.'

'Tell us about Louise,' Simon said quietly. 'Everything you know about her.'

'She is—was—his housekeeper and was here before I arrived, but I am not sure for how long. She was efficient and liked by the staff, some of whom live in the town and come up every day sharing an old car or on motor bikes which are parked on the edge of the forest outside the walls. There is a door there, but nobody is supposed to enter or leave it that way without Albert's permission. Morning or evening is the same. They are well-paid slaves … Louise and I live in the house. Her rooms are like these. We are comfortable enough, but Schengen does not want us to go out together as one of us must always be on duty. Louise has to go to Vianden sometimes to the shops and about staff. She has friends there—a married couple who keep a shop, I believe—but I do not know them. Louise has been kind to me because I am lonely. I like her very much, but sometimes I have felt that there is something about her I do not know. I cannot understand *why* she likes to be here when she is so experienced and clever that she could do a wonderful job in a big hotel … And before I tell you what has happened to her, I must tell you about me, else you will wonder why I am here.'

Simon was patient and let her tell her story in her own way.

Her mother was Spanish and her father English and she had no brothers or sisters. They lived in London, but her parents were both killed in an air disaster about a year ago. Maria, at the time of the tragedy, was at the end of a first-class secretarial course, and as she could speak French, Italian and Spanish as well as English she was well qualified for a top job and decided to look for work out of England and start life afresh. An advertisement in *The Times* introduced her to Schengen. The prospect of an exciting new life with artistic people where she could use her languages was tempting and the salary was fantastic.

'Paul warned me that the money was a substitute for a certain amount of freedom. If I took the job—and I admit that he flattered me—I was to realize that I should not get a holiday for a year. He told me about his plans for books and publishing and these interested me; he promised that I would work only for him and that every aspect of it all was absolutely confidential. I was a fool and took the job. I was alone in the world and this seemed a chance in a million, and so indeed it is, but any job would have been better, and I believe now that I should have run away if it had not been for Louise, who befriended me. Anyway I should have felt a coward if I hadn't stuck it out for a year. It is only during the last six months that Paul has put up the revolting pictures in the salon and on the walls. Most of them are by the red-bearded Dutchman, Dirck, who stayed here with a woman for several weeks. You saw him this evening. He is foul, but typical of most of the guests at these occasional weekend parties.'

'Yes, we understand all this, but you must tell us now more about Louise,' Simon interrupted. 'Did you ever discuss this sort of thing with her? Did she ever ask *you* questions about Schengen and your work for him?'

Maria hesitated. 'Yes—she did. She seemed to think that Paul was working on something else besides the book, but he wasn't with me. He has always behaved himself with me personally, and it was some time before he asked me to hostess his parties. Lately I've wondered what he does when he's not actually working on a book, but he seems to be obsessed with meeting new people. You might think that he'd be particularly interested in women, but he has a lot more men here too and not all are artistic types. Some stay two or three nights, but only those who are interested in books or pictures and may be of use to him have anything to do with my work. Many days I haven't enough to do …'

'Tell us more about Louise,' Simon insisted. 'You said, or implied, that she had a secret and was murdered because of it. We cannot help you unless you tell us the truth. What is Schengen really doing? Why does he have these extravagant parties? What is his secret discovered by Louise?'

'I cannot be sure. Don't bully me, Simon. I can't stand it … This is an evil house. Paul's weekend guests are either wicked to begin with or become converted after several visits. Louise once told me that she believes this house to be connected with secret passages through the rock to the old cellars of the château above. She believed that Schengen is a Satanist and that the people you saw tonight will celebrate a black mass tomorrow night, and that, by this means, he gets many people in his power. She knows now that he has another secret. The other day, after our interview, when he gave her his instructions about this weekend, she realized that as soon as she got back to her room, she had forgotten to ask him something important. She went back to what he calls his "Power House"—the ugly room where you saw him this morning—'

'The room with the goat's head on the wall,' Simon whispered. 'Yes, go on.'

Maria nodded. 'Louise told me that she had not closed the door properly and was about to knock and walk in when she heard men's voices. Nobody had passed her in the corridor and she was so surprised that she stopped and listened. Once before she told me that she believed there was more than one hidden door in that room. She did not tell me Paul's exact words. She was terrified, but it was something like—'Here are the complete details for May Day. They will all be given their orders tomorrow after the worship to our lord who has ordained this victory.' Louise must have been very brave. I cannot understand how she found the courage, but she opened the door a few more inches so that she could see into the room. Two men had their backs to her. One was Schengen, who was reaching up doing something to the goat's head. She said it was the door to a hidden safe which swung back with a click. His companion was Albert. She did not see his face but she did hear him reply in a language she could not understand. She knew, as I did, that Albert was Paul's sort of watchdog and spy. We both loathed him, so I can understand how Louise felt as she stood there alone not daring to move. She was so frightened that when she did step back she stumbled and fell against the door which opened wide.

'She told me that Paul was then sitting in his chair and Albert was so surprised he just goggled at her with his piggy eyes. It was then that Louise was so brave. She must have been, because she tried to make a joke of not closing the door properly before, and without taking any notice of Albert, asked Paul the question, about the housekeeping, got her answer, apologized about the door again and got out as quickly as she could. I met her on her way back and could see how upset she was and brought her in here and she told me what I've told you. You must both understand that I have only done this because you must get me out of here before they find out that you know. When they realize that you know, you may well be in danger, so why don't you both escape and take me with you. *I must get out!'*

As her voice rose hysterically, Rosina put a hand over her mouth and tried to comfort her. Then Simon, amazed at his luck, pressed her a little further.

'We'll find a way of helping you, Maria. I'm sure you are safe while we are with you. Keep your voice down and tell me whether you are sure that they know that Louise told you what she heard. What happened after she had told you all about it? Did Albert or Paul question either of you and do they suspect that she told you all about it? And when and how do you think they murdered her?'

'Too many questions!' Maria sobbed. 'Please let me alone now.'

Rosina glared a warning at Simon and then spoke quietly to Maria. 'Listen carefully, dear. We do want to help you and I have an idea that we can get you away in the morning. I'll tell you about it if you will help Simon by telling him what he wants to know. Remember that he is here because he is Paul's publisher. You, of all people, can see how important this is to him.'

But now Maria was not quite so sure of herself. She did not think that Albert or Paul knew for certain that Louise had told her the full story, but she was sure they suspected it. Both knew that they were friends.

'Albert couldn't stop me doing my job and I do know that soon after Louise had told me everything she went down to Vianden. She told me when we passed each other in one of the corridors that she was going to see her friends for half an hour. She probably got a lift down on the motor bike of one of the waiters. I haven't asked any of them and I'm not going to do so. All the staff liked her and I suspect that they all find ways of getting past Albert. When she said she was going to see her friends I wondered if she would ever come back. I have not seen her today.'

'Who told you she was dead?'

'In the kitchens they have been talking about the body of a woman found in the river. One of them said that Albert was asking for her and that frightened me.'

'How do you not know that Louise may have been so frightened that she drowned herself rather than come back here?'

'If she did, that would really be murder … I know that Albert is responsible because he told me so.'

Rosina got off the bed and stood by Simon.

'Yes, he did. I asked him if he knew where she was. He replied "She is dead. They found her in the river. Orders were given that no member of the staff was to leave this house until the weekend guests have gone. I have asked the master and that applies also to you. Orders must be obeyed lest accidents occur …" That is what he said. Louise was too brave to kill herself. I am sure that Albert found that she had gone to Vianden, waited for her to return and then abducted her and threw her in the river. There is a high place through the forest not far from here. We may never again see the man who took her on his bike. We shall never have any troubles over enquiries from the police. The head of them was at the party tonight and will be here tomorrow … Now I have told you all I know. Albert himself told me my friend was dead and as good as admitted that he was responsible. He knows that Louise must have seen the goat's head open. He suspects that she overheard Schengen's secret and he knows that Louise was the only friend I have here and that she may have told me. Paul probably shared his suspicion, and of course Louise would not have been killed without his permission.

'Now, do you see my danger? I have been warned not to leave Les Pins, but you must see that I dare not stay here. I have given you my trust. I have money but no car. You probably have both, but I warn you that you are both in danger here. Schengen wants something more from you than help in a new publishing business. I believe you should leave as soon as possible and take me with you ... I must know now. Will you help me?'

She covered her face with her hands again and Rosina saw the tears trickling through her fingers. Simon stood up, but before he could speak she said,

'Yes Maria. We believe you and will help you to escape. I have a plan. I will get you out of here in a few hours' time. I am not afraid of Paul Schengen. He cannot keep me here against my will. He knows we have friends staying in Vianden and I intend to visit them tomorrow morning after telling him so. You will come with me, hidden in the back of the car until we are out of here. Don't worry any more, and if you like I'll spend what's left of the night down here with you.'

11

The Great Bear

On the same Saturday morning, only a few hours after the events in Les Pins described in the last chapter, Marston Baines and Jake were enjoying a late breakfast over the Pop Shop in Luxembourg.

'Yes, Jake, this wandering round the Duchy and Ardennes in the decrepit vehicle Jan Schmidt gave me, has been worth while. As you had no special news for me last night, I assume that you are still waiting to hear from young Simon or your man in Vianden. Since I saw you I've met a few more of Schmidt's volunteers. I'm impressed, and suggest that you either ring Vianden or, if you prefer, I'll go over and see him. I know you realize how difficult it is to get news out of Les Pins ... I told you last night, I believe, that I finished my tour at Brussels to see Schmidt again. I am still not certain whether he suspects, or is even sure, about my double life. He is a clever and forceful character and dedicated to the cause of La Promesse. I'm sure we can use him, Jake, but only if there is a sudden emergency. I suppose you would have to get authority from London for that? And I suppose Schmidt will have to know who we are? I have told him that I will help him with propaganda and he presses me to pay a country visit to Les Pins, but we don't care for that idea, do we?'

Jake did not answer that question but asked another.

'Any more news about the corpse found in the river?'

'No doubt the woman was employed as housekeeper at Les Pins. The man Philippe whom I met, and to whom the woman reported when she could, identified her. Apparently there were no signs of physical violence on the body, but that doesn't mean much in these days. There are plenty of drugs available to operators like Schengen, and she could have been thrown in the river which runs round the hill on which the château is built. She may have been waylaid in the forest on her way back to Les Pins, but Schmidt's man suggests that the police won't be making many enquiries. Schengen's local influence is very strong.'

At this point the warning buzzer sounded and Jake said, 'Come down with me. This may be the message from Vianden.'

It was. Jake handed Marston spare headphones as he fitted his own and announced his code number. Latour's voice was clear.

'Vianden here. Miss Conway has just arrived, with Schengen's secretary with vital news from Les Pins. This girl claims that there is a meeting tonight of representatives of the May Day operation and that she knows where the documents and instructions are hidden. This information was given her by the woman whose body was recovered from the river. Miss Conway says that Simon Baines has approved this rescue operation, while he remains at Les Pins, but gave her instructions to report fully to me. The other girl is in distress, fearing for her life if she is caught, and begs to be taken to Belgium. Miss Conway's friends, Mr and Mrs Hand, are here at the hotel with their car. I suggest that they come to you at once, bringing Miss Conway and the girl Maria. Baines stresses that the situation is urgent and that action against Les Pins should be taken this evening …'

There was a pause here until Jake spoke. 'Nice work, Jean. Tell them to come at once. Miss Conway to leave her car with you. Let me know if Schengen bothers you, and if possible get somebody to keep an eye on Les Pins, and take a note of all cars arriving there. Further instructions later.'

He switched off and turned to Marston.

'Your lad and his girl seem to have been well trained. I'll report to London now and tell him you're here. If after we've both interviewed the girl secretary we are satisfied she's telling the truth, I'm going to get permission to raid the place tonight when the gang are inside. We may never again get a chance like this. I shall have to square the Government here, but I doubt if their help will be official. They know about La Promesse and that we don't like Schengen and what he is up to. For political reasons I'm sure they would rather blame a raid on Schmidt's boys than on us or any other foreign power. If it comes off, and it must, they'll be glad to share in the exposure of May Day and get Schengen out of the way for good ... Once we've cleaned up that hell-hole I hope they'll blow it up ... I'm glad to have you here, Marston and I'll see that they don't order you back to London. We'll take the risk and tell Schmidt at once that we may want his lads to break into Les Pins tonight. I take it that you have warned him that he might soon have a chance of showing his teeth and dealing with Schengen at the same time?'

Marston nodded. 'He'll enjoy this exercise. We can trust him. Many of his boys have done military service and I'm satisfied they're disciplined. Yes, leave him to me. The sooner the better. Not very comfortable for young Simon up there when Schengen realizes that Rosina has got the other girl away ... I suppose you suggested they use the Hands' car instead of Simon's which Schengen might be able to describe and get stopped somewhere?'

'Yes, I thought of that. Just one more point, Marston, and I must mention this to London. Surely you will have to tell Schmidt that you are now acting in an official capacity? Bit awkward isn't it?'

'Not really. I think he has always suspected. I shall assume he knows, and anyway he'd work with anybody who will help him to get Schengen and break up his gang. Let me telephone him from upstairs—I've got his special number—and you work on London from here. Be tough with Pendent and tell him we can't miss this opportunity. Another thing. We must get young Simon out of there as soon as we can, but we'll get more news of his situation from his girl. What do you do about your shop on days like this when you're really busy?'

'Put a notice on the door—"Closed today. Please ring bell". This is rather a special one-man business! I'll see to it.'

Marston felt the old thrill when he spoke to Schmidt. He was back in action and once again engaged in the war against the forces of evil. Schmidt at once accepted his authority without question.

'You can take it, Marston, that unless I hear to the contrary within three hours, four coachloads of shock troops, who we call "tourists", will be outside the gates of Les Pins prepared to break in and take action after dark. We shall try to avoid action which is too rough because the occupants of the house are, for the present, more use to us alive than dead. If we are to have other official assistance in clearing up the mess, you are making the necessary arrangements and will let me know. La Promesse prefers to work independently but is always at the service of law and order. That is understood?'

Marston agreed.

'I'm sure your tourists will be appreciated, but as I am not so certain that more official sources will take the same view, it would be advisable for your men to take with them appliances which will facilitate their quick entry. Yes, Jan. I expect to be there and shall be accompanied. Good luck. If you want me later ring this number, but don't leave it too late. And this is important. I am expecting a refugee from Les Pins in about half an hour. She is, was rather, Schengen's secretary and friend of your Louise. As soon as I have questioned her I should like her to be in the care of Madame Schmidt. She can be brought by car by two of my young friends who can be trusted. You will realize that having escaped from Les Pins she is in fear of her life. Louise gave her the information we all need. Please care for her until she knows what she wants to do. I will tell her you are friends.'

And so it was left. Jake came up with the news that Peter Pendent was impressed by the latest developments, amused about Marston and La Promesse, but under the circumstances willing that they should work together to get Schengen and the information about May Day.

'As I thought, Marston, he doesn't want to give us official permission at this stage to blow the place up because Luxembourg is a sovereign state. I've explained that we must act tonight, and I'm sure that if we get what we want the officials will do the explaining after. Anyway I've told him and he hasn't stopped us. Not so important, but they have checked up on Timothy Hitchens. He's not considered very satisfactory and is under observation. Peter suggests that his presence at Les Pins is worth investigation. When these young friends of yours arrive, I'd be glad if you'd take command. They know you and it will save time.'

Marston nodded. 'That's true, but I think we must question both the girls together. I want you present when Rosina tells her story. You haven't met her yet, and possibly you're not too happy about her working in with Simon. I know the girl, and have seen her under pressure, so I'm a little prejudiced in her favour. We must both be sure that the girl who has escaped—a girl probably much more under Schengen's influence than the one they murdered—really is a defector. It is just possible they are using her to find me. I doubt it, but I am on the wanted list. We think it a sign of strength that Simon and I should both use our own names, but these people are cunning. Meanwhile the sooner we are inside that place the better I shall be pleased. Maybe I'm getting old and nervy, but young Simon is very much alone if Maria's escape is genuine.'

Jake had no immediate answer to this and was relieved by the ringing of the door bell.

'They don't know you're here, do they? Like to let them in yourself?'

Marston smiled. 'No thanks. Go and make your own judgements.'

Jake left the door at the bottom of the stairs open so that Marston could hear.

'Good morning,' he heard Charles Hand say. 'We're sorry to bother you when your shop is closed. We come from Jean Latour in Vianden. He wants a cassette of Marlene Dietrich singing "Where Have All the Flowers Gone?" He assured me that we would get the best service here.'

'I hope so,' Jake replied. 'Please go straight up. The proprietor is waiting for you.'

Marston heard the shop door close and footsteps on the stairs. He stepped forward as Charles stood aside for the girls to come in. Rosina was first. She was wearing a blue jersey and jeans. Her hair was in disarray, her face without makeup, streaked with dust. When she saw Marston her tired eyes widened with disbelief, and at that moment the tough old bachelor felt his own eyes sting with tears, as he realized what she must be suffering for the cause which he and Simon served.

'Marston?' she whispered unbelievingly. 'It's really you! We thought you were kidnapped or something awful, and all the time you were near us. You always are when you're wanted most. Oh darling Marston, I'm so tired.'

Suddenly she was in his arms with her face pressed against his old tweed jacket. Maria, looking exhausted and bewildered, was just behind and it was Kate who then took control. She held out a hand to Marston.

'We should have guessed you were in this game. Jean Latour is on your side of course. Lovely to see you again anyway. May we sit down? And if somebody will lead me to the kitchen I'll make coffee for us all. We need it. Hot, black, and possibly with a dash of brandy.'

'I'm the boss of the kitchen,' Jake said. 'Bring your husband and Maria with you, while Marston and I hear Rosina's story first. Listen, Maria. You are safe now. Marston and I will talk to you when you have rested, but we've already made arrangements to take you to Brussels where you will be looked after by friends who have no reason to like Paul Schengen.'

She smiled at him tearfully.

'Thank you. I am very tired but will tell you all I know when you are ready. I am lucky with my friends and I trust you all. I should like to go to Brussels.'

Then she turned to Marston who gently disengaged himself from Rosina and smiled at her.

'You are Marston Baines. Simon's uncle. I do not know how or why you are here, but *please* get Simon out of that place. I am sure he is in great danger.'

When Jake returned from the kitchen, Rosina was sitting next to Marston on the sofa. She seemed to have recovered and said at once,

'I'm told that I am to call you Jake. You know who I am and will have heard Maria's story from Jean Latour. Marston says you must hear it again from her. That's fine. I'm certain that she is telling the truth. You needn't waste time telling me that Marston and you and the Latours are on the same side. So is Simon, and he's on his own now, and Maria is right that he's in danger.'

Jake nodded. 'We know that. We've been busy since Latour reported. Now tell us quickly how you got out with Maria. Presumably she told you of her fears last night?'

Rosina told the story of Maria's dramatic appeal to them at the party, and how they had discussed her escape in her bedroom.

'I was fairly sure that Simon was still on his guard about her, but I was certain that she was genuine and that what she told us about Louise was true. Anyway, Schengen and his horrible bully Albert had murdered Louise, and threatened Maria—but she will tell you about that—and I suddenly saw a way of getting her out and told her in front of Simon. Of course I can drive Simon's car. It's one of those with room for lots of luggage behind the back seat. You know it, Marston. You can fit a cover over the bags and there's a lift-up door at the back. Maria is small and I thought she could hide there for a few minutes until we got away from Les Pins. Although that pig Albert can open the big gates automatically, I hoped I could persuade Paul Schengen to let me go out in the morning to visit Charles and Kate at La Fôret. He met them in London and knew they were our friends, and he had once suggested that he would like them here as guests. Visitors' cars are parked at the side of the house, out of sight of the front door.

'Maria was excited about this plan, and was sure she could escape through the kitchen and get into the boot of the car. We fixed a time—we've only had about four hours' sleep—and although I offered to stay with Maria in her room because she was in such a state, Simon wouldn't let me. There was nobody about when we went to our rooms. Simon woke me as arranged. Only a waiter was in the dining room, but we managed to swallow some coffee. It was nearly the time we had arranged with Maria, so Simon said he would see if the front door was open yet, and I was left alone with about a million butterflies fluttering round in my tummy. We decided that if possible, even if the big gates were open, I wouldn't drive out unless we had seen Paul and told him I was going to meet Charles and Kate. Luck was with us. I don't know where Simon found Paul because there wasn't a chance for him to tell me, but he was probably in the hall with Albert. Simon brought Paul, who was wearing a fantastic, oriental dressing-gown thing. Simon was super. He said: "I told Paul that you're going down to Vianden to have a day with Charles and Kate, but that I can't come. I'll bring the car round for you now."'

Here she paused for breath. Marston nodded approvingly and

Jake murmured, 'And then no doubt you got to work on Paul?'

'I wouldn't put it quite like that. I thanked him for his lovely party last night, and said that although I wanted Simon to come too, I knew it wasn't fair to take him away from discussing important business. And then I thanked him again for giving us this wonderful chance of a new, exciting job, and told him that I would tell Charles and Kate about the marvellous party.'

'And what did he say to that?' Marston asked.

'He reminded me that there was another very special party tonight with artistic friends and critics from other European countries, and I must be sure to be back in time, and that one day soon he would like to meet Charles and Kate, but tonight was rather special because everybody would be masked. Maria says it's a black mass and not for the first time, but you must ask her about it. Well, that's all really. He came out to the door with me and Albert was there looking like thunder, and when I wished him good morning and said what a lovely day it was going to be, I could see his fat neck going red ... Then my darling Simon drove up and when he got out and I got in, he gave me a quick kiss and whispered that Maria was in the back and I drove through those awful gates, and in the mirror I saw them close behind me. As soon as we were in the forest I stopped and let Maria out so that she could sit with me. She was in rather a state, and I don't blame her, do you? The Latours were kind. Simon told me that Jean would know what to do as soon as I told him what had happened ... That's it really, except that the most wonderful thing in my life after Simon is having Marston here. You'll look after Simon, won't you Marston?'

'Yes, my dear. We will. I know I speak for Jake when we say that you are a brave girl—but of course I always knew that. I have one more question to ask. Several times you have mentioned Schengen's manservant, Albert. Obviously an unpleasant type. Can you describe him?'

'He's horrible. The most ugly man I've ever seen. Big and stout. Absolutely bald, shiny clean-shaven white skin, small piggy eyes. Always dressed in black. Hardly ever speaks. Must have rubber soles to his shoes because you never hear him coming. Sometimes when you're talking to somebody, when you look round he's there. When he has spoken to us he uses rather stately English—like a butler in an old-fashioned play. Somehow you feel that it's what he *doesn't* say that matters. I'm sure he spies on the staff and guests and I think, but I'm not sure because I haven't been there long enough, that he is often with Paul Schengen. Maria is sure he murdered Louise but she'll tell you about that. I hate him. He is an evil man … May I go now, please? I'm tired and if Charles and Kate are going to take Maria to Brussels, I would rather stay here, with you both, before we go back to Les Pins and fetch Simon. And soon, please.'

'Thank you, Rosina. I'm proud to know you. Go and rest on Marston's bed. Up the stairs and first door on the right.'

'Yes,' Jake said when Rosina had gone. 'You're right. Courage as well as nerve. Now for Maria. You're the kindly uncle type, so you start off and put her at ease and I'll take over. I don't doubt that Rosina's judgement is right, but we must be sure. Anyway if we get her to Brussels, Schmidt's people will keep an eye on her, until we've cleared up the mess here.'

Marston agreed. 'Fair enough. I've got something nagging at the back of my mind, Jake. When the chance comes, ask Maria for a description of the bully Albert. See if it's the same as Rosina's. She's known him longer.'

Maria told her story well. Marston made it clear that he, Simon, Rosina and Jake were on the same side and eager to clean up Les Pins as soon as possible. He realized that if, by some remote chance, she was working for Schengen it would not matter because she would be in the care of the Schmidts in Brussels until the raid was over. There was still time to warn Jan with a message carried by Charles that she should not be allowed to go off on her own until they were all sure.

Jake questioned her shrewdly about her work for Schengen. Had she any suspicion that he was doing anything else besides his writing and photography and plans for his own publishing? She maintained, as she had to Simon and Rosina, that he had never asked her to do anything else but help him with his investigations and plans for these projects. 'But,' she added under pressure, 'I have wondered why he needed all those mechanical things and gadgets. When Louise told me about the goat's head safe I wondered what secrets he kept there. I know now, but not then. I sometimes wondered why he had so many strangers at these "arty" weekends, but I do know that he was quite famous in the artistic world and supposed to be very advanced with the paintings he collected and displayed there.'

They asked her whether she had ever been to a black mass and she shook her head.

'No. I realize now that early on, even at my first interview, he made some vague suggestions that I pretended not to understand. I knew a girl in London who got caught up in Satanism and was soon in real trouble. I think Schengen had the sense to see that I wasn't interested, and that it was safer from his point of view to keep me out of it. He was correct in his behaviour to me. He paid me well, he didn't like me going out but I had promised to stay a year. And then Louise was my friend ... The worst thing about Les Pins was the brute Albert.'

This was their chance.

She described his physical appearance as Rosina had done, but because she had known him for months she was able to give them more valuable information.

'I have never understood the relationship between the two men. He was Schengen's personal servant, if there is such a thing in these days, but I do not think he was interested in the art world. He was a bully to the staff who hated him, but I have always had the feeling that there was something between the two men. Something perhaps from the past? He hated me—a sort of jealousy, perhaps—but I was always surprised that he and Schengen did quite often meet in the office. Albert spied on the staff and on visitors and I am not surprised that he murdered Louise. There *is* something, some secret shared by those two men, that I do not understand.'

'Do you think that Albert had anything to do with the black mass goings on?' Marston asked.

'Possibly, yes. I'm sure there are secret connections between Les Pins and the dungeons of the ruined château above. Louise agreed. There is probably an old chapel there where they celebrate their mass. When there is one of these, I've noticed that Albert is always missing from the house. I don't know what Rosina has said to you about him, but Albert terrifies me … You are going to help me get away aren't you?'

They reassured her and as soon as she had gone back to the others in the kitchen, Marston turned to Jake.

'Do you realize we may be on to something even bigger than we thought? You may not remember, Jake, but at least ten years ago most of our European friends were in a tizzy about a KGB operator who moved from country to country organizing sabotage. He was amazingly successful and all our branches and agencies were urged to track him down and deal with him. Then he vanished. Some said he had been recalled to his motherland. The CIA in America was warned to look out for him. He was looked for in Cuba, in southeast Asia and even in Ireland to see if he was helping the IRA. He disappeared, but sabotage, as we know, continued. I believe we have found him. The physical description still fits. We never knew how many different names he worked under but he was known to us all as The Great Bear. You must check with London at once, but I am almost certain his biography will prove that he is a renegade priest—and that fits in with the black mass. Get on to London, Jake.

Tell Peter Pendent what I suspect, and that Schengen is under the orders and control of The Great Bear who deliberately vanished because he knew we were all after him.'

12

Simon Alone

As soon as Rosina had driven out of Les Pins with her precious cargo, Simon went back into the hall. Albert, after turning the switch which closed the gates, walked away after a brief word with Paul.

'Sorry if I disturbed you just now,' Simon said. 'We didn't have a chance last night to tell you that Rosina had promised her friends to spend today with them, but she particularly wanted me to find you and explain. In fact she said she wouldn't go until we had seen you. I haven't had much chance to think over our talk yesterday, your hospitality and party is reason for that, but I would be grateful if you could spare me some more time later. Would that be possible?'

'Yes, Simon, it would. I have more to say to you also. If you are going up to your room now I'll telephone, or ask Albert to let you know when I'm ready. I have a busy day before me but I have not changed my mind about the importance of our collaboration. I will see you later.'

Simon knew that he too had a busy day before him. He was thankful that Rosina would soon be safe with Latour. Charles and Kate would be available and he was sure that, between them, they would take Rosina and Maria to Jake in Luxembourg. It then occurred to him that Paul's suggestion that he should go to his room to await a summons was out of character. Not quite as friendly as yesterday?

When he opened the door of his room, Timothy Hitchens was sitting on his bed. But not the suave, well-dressed Timothy of last night. Although wearing a gay dressing gown over his pyjamas, he looked a wreck. His head was in his hands and when he lowered them his fingers were shaking uncontrollably. His face was yellow and his eyes red-rimmed. Simon knew that he was either drugged or suffering from a severe hangover.

'Hullo, old boy. Jus' thought I'd like a little chat. Not too good this morning ... Been worrying about you, Simon. Been thinking 'bout you two—'bout your lovely Rosina. Worried. Hope you don't mind a little chat, ol' boy. Not so many Brits here this weekend and we've got to stick together ... Know what I mean, Simon?'

Simon didn't, but there wasn't much he could do about this situation except to keep him talking and give him two aspirins. He did both and eventually realized that poor Timothy was trying to make a confession—and possibly to get some information in return.

First he asked once more if Simon had ever been here before and whether he had 'taken the oath'. On being assured that he had not, he began to blubber, and eventually admitted that Schengen, with Albert's help, supplied drugs to those of his guests who wanted them.

'And I've got to have my shot, old boy. I must have it now. He won't give it me until I've found out about you. I find out about people for him you see ... I do it in London ... I find out things for Kathie too ... I met her in London. Kathie has been good to me, but she hates the Brits. Now Paul wants to know more about you. He thinks you can help him to find out more 'bout that old uncle of yours. Don't really know why, but I don't think he likes him ... And then there's this wonderful worship and the things we do at the mass. There's one tonight and he'll give me all I want before we start at midnight, but I can't wait. I want it now. And because of this you must tell me about Marston Baines ... I'm relying on you to help me, old boy.'

There was not much satisfaction for Simon in the realization that Paul's hunch about Marston was well-founded. Suddenly it occurred to him that if this room was bugged—and he had assumed that it was, although he had not discovered anything—Timothy was too drunk, or ill, to have remembered such a possibility. Already he had virtually betrayed Schengen.

'I'd help you if I could, Tim,' he said. 'I don't really understand what you're talking about, and I can't see why Paul wants to know more about Marston. He's still working down in Sussex, doing well with his thrillers. I think I told you that my firm publish him. If I were you I'd go back to bed for a bit, and try to pull yourself together. Forget this conversation and so will I. What you've just said is nothing to do with me. I'm here on publishing business and I'm not really interested in the other people here. I'm going to see Paul soon, and if we can finish our talk this morning I'm thinking of leaving Les Pins with Rosina to spend the rest of my leave with her and our friends down in Vianden. We might go to Holland. I've always wanted to see Amsterdam. I've plenty of work in London, too. Pull yourself together, Tim. I'll keep your secret. Have you talked all this over with your girl-friend Kathie?'

Tim staggered to his feet and made no answer to the last question. Simon helped him into his room and when he got back to his own the telephone was buzzing.

'Schengen here. I'm ready for you now. Come down to the Power House.'

This was more of an order than a request and Simon began to feel apprehensive. He was thankful that Rosina was well out of it. He had no doubts about Latour and was sure that as soon as he had contacted Jake in Luxembourg, the two girls with Charles and Kate would be on their way to safety.

Simon was in no doubt that he was in danger. It would not be long before Maria was missed and somebody might have noticed her going out to the car—or even getting into it. He had only checked that she was in the boot before driving round to the courtyard. Somehow or other he must get the evidence from the safe behind the goat's head, although that might have been moved—or destroyed. He might have to pretend to defect and to give Paul false information, but that would be risky because he might get nothing worthwhile in return … The seconds were ticking by. Paul sounded impatient and angry, and suddenly Simon decided that his only course was to go on playing the innocent, ambitious young publisher and to hope that when Maria was safe, Jake would plan an attack and a rescue this evening. Certainly Rosina would stop at nothing to get him out of Les Pins. He wished that he knew what had happened to Marston and how he would have played this sort of game. Suddenly he knew the answer. Marston would have played it through to the end, never forgetting that by thought, word or deed, before anything else, he was a writer in search of copy. He must act the same way, and be nothing but Schengen's publisher. Then he remembered he was still carrying the small gun Jake had given him. He wished that he had given this to Rosina to dispose of, but all that he could do now was to hide it under some of his clothes still in his suitcase.

The door of the 'Power House' was closed and did not open until he knocked politely. Paul was sitting behind his desk with Albert standing behind him with his shaven head on a level with the goat's hideous mask. Paul asked him to sit down.

Simon looked meaningly at Albert and remained standing.

'I'm sorry, Paul. I didn't realize you were engaged. Would you like me to wait outside?'

'No. No. Sit down. Albert is interested in our publishing plans and I want him to know what we are discussing. There are times when I have found his advice very sound.'

Simon didn't care for this, but he sat and took a good look at Albert who returned his interest with an insolent stare. Rosina was right. Albert was not only ugly in his person but repulsive in a more subtle way. He gave an impression of hatred, and Simon remembered that Maria had described him as 'evil'. His small cold eyes now fixed on him were hypnotic, and he felt a shiver of apprehension as he realized that the man was not going to leave the room. For the first time he sensed real, unspoken antagonism from the manservant. And Schengen's attitude was certainly not cordial.

Simon asked, 'What was it you particularly wanted to discuss first, Paul? I think we agreed on the general contents of the new book and, as I told you yesterday, I am looking forward to working here. I have plenty of ideas for our publishing plans, but I would like to think that these must be confidential between the two of us, and we can't discuss these in detail until we have fixed the terms of my engagement. And I would like to know in more detail what my duties and responsibilities will be.'

'Quite so,' Schengen agreed. 'We also have to agree on some other matters. I agree that further details of the new book can be discussed later, but you can strengthen my belief in your future if you will prove, by answering a few questions about people known to both of us, that our ideas for the future of a progressive society are enthusiastically shared.'

'I'm not sure what you mean, sir,' but before Paul could answer, the sinister Albert uttered one word—'Hitchens'.

And then Simon knew. His conversation with Timothy had, as he suspected, been overheard. Surely nothing that he had said to Timothy was incriminating, but what Timothy had said to him would not do that pathetic failure much good.

Then the telephone on Paul's desk buzzed and as he announced himself and listened, Simon saw his face change. It was as if a mask, portraying a cultured and artistic patron of the arts, had been torn off, exposing the master of Les Pins in all his villainy.

As he replaced the receiver he turned to Albert who moved

behind Simon's chair. Schengen opened a drawer in his desk and took out what looked like a small water pistol. As he lifted the weapon his fingers were shaking with rage.

'Listen to me carefully, young Baines. This pistol is charged with a new nerve gas in the form of vapour. A small dose will immobilize you and a larger one will kill without leaving a trace. It has been tested recently with complete success and I will use it now if you show any resistance. In case you may be tempted to move, Albert will save your life by holding you firmly in your chair. I have just had a message from a trustworthy member of my kitchen staff who, when on his way to work this morning, saw Maria sitting next to Miss Conway in her car. He admits that he heard a car coming down through the forest and had the sense to hide behind a tree until it had passed. He was curious to see who was about so early in the morning after last night's festivities—'

'Don't be ridiculous, Paul,' Simon interrupted. 'Tell this man to take his hands off me and put away that silly toy. Maybe one of your sneaking kitchen spies did see Maria in Miss Conway's car. No doubt she was walking down to the town and Rosina gave her a lift. That was the natural, courteous thing to do. And why should one of your servants want to hide and make a report to you? This house is not a prison, is it? Surely your secretary is allowed out of here?'

'So?' Schengen said quietly. 'I am not here to answer your questions, and you must understand that *you* are now in a situation when you have to answer mine. Where has that girl of yours taken Maria?'

'How should I know? How can you be sure that your spy is telling the truth? I don't know how you treat your servants, but it could be that this one wants to ingratiate himself with you. Anyway, you know where Miss Conway was going. She told you herself. She is going to La Fôret to spend a day with our friends. And I must remind you that after your hysterical treatment of me, the chances of us working together in publishing are now very remote … Anyway, telephone the hotel now and ask for Miss Conway … And do put that silly thing away.'

'Let us see how it works, shall we?' Schengen whispered. 'Hold him down, Albert.'

Simon had no chance. As Schengen leaned across the desk and sent a puff of vapour into his face he could not even struggle. He could see and hear but there was no strength in his limbs. He could not even protest when Albert lifted his arms and secured them with handcuffs. The steel was not even cold on his wrists, but strangely enough his sense of hearing seemed keener than normal.

He watched Schengen lift his telephone and dial. Then he spoke in French and announced himself as a friend of Miss Conway who would like to speak to her if convenient. As Albert had now left the room, Simon could hear Latour's answer.

'Alas, Monsieur, Miss Conway is not now staying at the hotel, but she called here about half an hour ago, but has gone out in their car with her friends who are staying here. No, Monsieur, there was nobody else with them … No, Monsieur, Miss Conway arrived alone. Would you care to leave a message? No, Monsieur. I do not know where they have gone but expect them to be back later in the day.'

Simon was sure that Rosina would have told Jean everything who obviously would lie about Maria, who would be brought to the hotel for safety's sake. He may even have guessed the identity of the caller.

Simon's speech was still blurred as he felt strength returning to his limbs, but he managed to say, 'What did I tell you, Paul? Your spy is probably lying and Rosina has done what we told you she was going to do … You must be crazy to behave like this. Surely that's what's wrong with you, Paul. You've been overworking. What's happened to you since we were talking together yesterday about the new book?'

Schengen looked at him pityingly and then his expression hardened and suddenly Simon feared that he really was going out of his mind. His situation was desperate enough without having to deal with a madman.

He was talking again now and making extravagant gestures with his hands.

'Until Maria is found and brought back here, I have decided that you also will be missing. I believe that you have much to tell me about the generally unknown activities of Peter Pendent in London and also your esteemed uncle Marston Baines. I am going to give you some hours of silent contemplation on these matters ... I had hoped that you would be willing to work for me of your own free will ... Make no mistake, you poor deluded boy, I shall find Maria who has betrayed my trust and deal with her as I recently dealt with another traitor. I shall find your girl and bring her back here as soon as possible. No doubt you will not wish to see her hurt or suffer any indignity.

'Let me explain. Tonight, at midnight in the secret chapel of the ancient château above us, there will be a celebration of our age-old worship to our lord and master. In his honour, and because he is all-powerful and will help those who acknowledge him, we shall offer him a blood sacrifice. Then he will strengthen his servants in their efforts in their fight to establish his kingdom on earth ... The sacrificial victim has been chosen. You know him, Baines. He was in your bedroom not long ago and had too much to say. A foolish, weak young man who has disappointed us. Sometimes we make mistakes. I hope we have not been wrong about you. At the moment we are not in need of a second sacrifice tonight, but I must tell you that Timothy is very poorly today. I hope he will last the day ... Meantime, Baines, I am going to introduce you to the dungeons of the great château of Vianden and there you will stay until you tell us the truth about Peter Pendent of London. You know what I mean. I am sure that you work for him in another capacity besides publishing. I am interested in your uncle also and you may be able to help us there. Miss Conway is another who, I am sure, could be helpful. If you would care to tell me where she might be found now, we might dispense with the dungeons for the present, but I am in rather a hurry as there is much to do before our celebrations tonight. I can spare some time now, Simon, if you would care to talk. Almost everything in life depends on which side we are on does it not? Do you want to talk now or would you prefer to think over the situation in the dungeons? Albert will show you the way.'

But Simon merely shrugged his shoulders and said nothing.

13

Sacrifice

Half an hour after Marston's disclosure that Albert was almost certainly an agent of the KGB, the two British agents were still discussing the situation. Jake had telephoned Peter Pendent in London, asking if he could confirm that the Soviet agent was still at large. Meanwhile Marston had told Jan in Brussels that Maria was safe and that the three young people were bringing her to Uccle as soon as they could get there. They were interrupted by Rosina.

'I can't rest properly until I've spoken to you both. I don't know your plans for this evening except that you will be going back to Les Pins. I know enough of what is happening to be sure there is going to be trouble. Simon is in danger. *I am not going to Brussels with the others.* I have got Maria out for you, and it is on her evidence that you can raid Les Pins. Apart from your own job, you have to rescue Simon. I am disgusted with myself for leaving him, although I am glad to have helped Maria. She has told me all she knows about the geography of the place, so I am the only person now outside who can tell you about the inside. I do not know when, or how, you are going to get in, but you will have to take me with you. I've told Charles I'm not going with him now, and you may like to know that he's coming back here with Kate just as soon as Maria is safe. They will expect to help you rescue Simon. I would like at least an hour's rest now, please, but I don't mind Marston waking me when you've made your plans … I've said goodbye to Maria … Don't either of you bother to get up. I can find my own way back.'

'Well, well,' Jake remarked inadequately as the door closed very firmly behind her. 'I see what you mean. Quite a girl, and it's true that she is the only one of us, including Jan Schmidt's lot, who knows the inside of Les Pins. We must take her. In your special care, Marston. What about the others?'

'I'll see that Charles is recruited by Jan, and perhaps we can arrange to put Kate in Rosina's care. I'm not keen in involving these youngsters in a mess like this, but they may be useful … Anyway let's see them on their way now.'

Maria was rather emotional when she tried to thank the two men, but Marston interrupted her. 'There is more than one way in which you can show your thanks, Maria. You are going to friends in Brussels and you will be in the care of a Madame Schmidt. She is English, and will know of your troubles. Her husband, who you may also see, holds the same views of Schengen and Albert as we do. You are to trust and obey them as you would us. They will help you eventually to go wherever you wish, but you are not to leave their house without their permission. Give them your confidence. And Maria, if you can remember whether there are any secret doors in Schengen's workroom or can answer any questions about Les Pins which the Schmidts may ask, you are to do so. They are your friends, as we are. So, goodbye my dear,' and then surprisingly, 'God bless you.'

Her eyes were brimming as she turned to Kate who led her from the room.

'Cheerio both,' Charles grinned. 'Kate and I will be back because tonight your ways shall be our ways. What will we do if we can't get into this shop?'

'Go to La Fôret in Vianden,' Jake said. 'Latour or Marguerite will have news for you. Good luck … Now, Marston, what else have you to say while we're waiting for the London call?'

'Have you had any experience of Satanism, witchcraft or the practice of black magic, Jake? In our job, I mean.'

'Not really. I know it exists. I know its power is growing both in Europe and America, and we now know that the Great Bear may be a practitioner apart from all his other interests or hobbies … Are you suggesting that he and Schengen are using it successfully now against us?'

'Yes, I am. Or rather, I suspect that the KGB are encouraging Albert to use it for recruiting and for infiltration. I did not dare to tell Rosina or the others what I fear we shall be up against tonight, or of my fears for Simon. I have occasionally been accused of moralizing, but I have had previous experience of these horrors, and you must be told what we may have to face in addition to the rough stuff which will be supplied by Jan Schmidt's bravos.'

Jake nodded. 'Go on. I'm not likely to accuse you of humbug, Marston. It's probably my loss not to have met you before.'

'What I have learned is that the practice of magic—either black or white—is more than a fad or a cult. It is a sort of science or art of willpower able to bring about change. A study of witchcraft supports this. Witches claimed to be able to kill from a distance by willpower. The use of magic throughout the world is age-old. Today it is growing because it brings the promise of power. Its natural enemy is Christianity, but what is important to us is to realize that a true Satanist does not even need a motive for murder, and has no scruples about offering a human sacrifice at a black mass. We can be reasonably certain now that Albert will be the celebrant at the performance tonight, which is a parody of the real mass and must be conducted by a priest who has revoked his office. I would think that tonight is to be a black mass for those who are to be the leaders in their own countries of the May Day demonstrations, who must all have time to get back to their respective base … Simon is at risk. I'm sure he won't leave the place without the evidence we want, and apparently the only clue he's got came from the dead girl with the suggestion that the goat's head in Schengen's room covers a safe.'

Jake agreed. 'But he won't be popular when they find out that both Maria and Rosina have disappeared, and that should be about now. Incidentally, I gave him one of our small guns before he left. Thought it might strengthen his morale.'

'His morale will stand up to most situations, but he'll never carry the gun while he is acting the eager young publisher ... No, Jake. Not just because he is my dead brother's son, not even because, in a way, I've got him into this, but because he's one of us. Remember that he could have got out with Rosina this morning ... When London gets through I'd like authority to get into Les Pins just as soon as I can get there. No reason why I shouldn't pay a fellow author a friendly visit. Natural enough, as I missed Peter Pendent's party in London. Obviously I should like to meet Simon and his girl as they're his guests. I'd be more use there than here, but this is your show, Jake, and I suppose you had better consult London.'

Jake looked thoughtful, but before he could reply the warning buzzed and he went to his control room.

The minutes dragged before he returned. Marston turned from the window where he had been watching the shadows of the leaves of the plane trees on the sunlit pavements below. It often seemed strange to him that millions of peaceful citizens in Western Europe took their freedom for granted.

'Sorry, Marston. So far as you are concerned, Peter is against you going to Les Pins before we all go tonight. He's been busy and efficient, and we're to go ahead with Schmidt and raid the place after dark. They insist that it is now more important to get the lot of them in one swoop. We assume, and I've said that you agree, that all the representatives of the various countries concerned are likely to be present. We'll get them before we concentrate on written evidence. I've told them about the black mass and Peter says you know all about that and he wants you to work closely with Schmidt. Suggest you telephone Brussels and offer to go over and help. Schmidt may have already arranged through his man in Vianden to have some watchers in the forest. Every car that arrives today is to be recorded. I want Jan to include some mechanics amongst his tourists who must immobilize every car after dark. He must bring locksmiths and experts on safe breaking. La Promesse has to get us in and do the technical stuff. You'd agree, wouldn't you, that the time to get them together is when they're at their disgusting parody of a mass?'

'Yes, the house should be empty then except possibly for a few servants, but we have yet to find where they meet. I would guess that what Maria called the "Power House" will help us. It is from there that entrances to passages through the rock might be found. Everything depends on us getting in with the minimum of noise and fuss. I believe that Albert is really the boss and that we may then assume that he will not be on guard at the door of the house as usual? It is also likely that before the ceremony, which I would guess will be held in the ancient underground chapel of the château, there will be a sort of drunken feast. Although dangerous for us to assume that they will be off their guard, I suggest that the best time for attack is between eleven and midnight … By the way, what was Peter's reaction to my hunch about the Great Bear? Any news filed away in the archives?'

'Sorry I didn't tell you. He thinks you could be right. Whatever happens tonight, we must get him—and be sure to carry a gun. As you must go to Brussels, I'll get you a fast car and ring Jan first. I must know his plans, and if he presses you about official backing, you can tell him that I have the promise of unofficial help in the background. Somebody has to make the arrests … What are you going to do with that girl now on your bed? You can't leave her here. I'm terrified of her.'

Marston's answering smile was grim. 'Get me that car. Give me

171

half an hour to fix up with Schmidt and then I'll take Rosina with me and tell her as much as is good for her. We'll all be back here by early evening unless there are complications in Brussels.'

Jake nodded. 'OK. You can forget being the shabby old author looking for copy, and just be yourself for twenty-four hours. Good luck! It's going to be a long day.'

It was certainly a long day for Simon.

After his first refusal to answer Schengen's ranting, he wondered whether the suave art expert and connoisseur who had been such a success in London was going off his head. Schengen's face was mottled, his hands clenched and unclenched on the desk and there was froth on his lips. His voice rose and shook with rage as he abused Simon for his silence.

'You fool, Baines. An insolent silence won't help you now. We intend to know where that sly girl of yours has taken my employee Maria who is under grave suspicion. No doubt she told you many lies yesterday about my friends. Unless you tell me where she can be found we shall have to persuade you to be helpful. Your pretended innocence does not impress me, and neither are we satisfied about your relationship with Hitchens whose conversation with you this morning is known to us … You don't understand your danger, Baines. Hitchens is now spending some time in meditation. He has failed us and has not much time left. I had hoped you would be one of our successes, but I fear that you are also a disappointment.'

There was nothing cheering for Simon in this outburst. How much did Schengen really know? Why a few references to Marston and Pendent? In the world of espionage Simon had already learned that the enemy invariably knew more than he was expected to know. To underestimate their intelligence was often fatal. But perhaps he could best outwit Schengen by playing the innocent?

'It's no use, Paul. I don't understand what you mean, or why I am sitting here in handcuffs as if I was a criminal. You know why

I'm here. I suppose it is possible that Rosina picked up Maria in the forest and gave her a lift to Vianden. If so, she probably put her down at her request before she went on to the hotel. You knew she was going with her friends. You've met them, but how should I know where they have gone? Do you usually handcuff your guests? Your behaviour is outrageous and inexcusable. It is not my fault that Timothy Hitchens came to my room this morning. You probably know that he is a drug addict—of course you do, and as you were listening to our conversation, you know that I know. I'm sorry for Timothy but he's nothing to do with me. I can't imagine why you want him here, unless it's something to do with his Irish girl-friend. She didn't seem to be interested in modern art! ... No, Mr Schengen. I cannot begin to guess the meaning of your extraordinary behaviour. Unlock these handcuffs and I will pack and go. Yesterday I thought that I should have enjoyed working with you on your new publishing proposition, but obviously that dream is over, and I cannot understand why we were invited here.'

Simon thought this to be quite a good effort. Nothing that he had said suggested that he was anything but an ambitious young publisher, but even as he watched Schengen take the vapour pistol from the drawer of his desk, he knew that he had no chance of escape. The man was a maniac, and when Simon looked up and saw the yellow eyes in the hideous goat's head staring down at him, he felt a sudden shudder of fear. Then he heard a sound behind him, but before he could turn, strong hands grasped the back of his neck and hauled him to his feet.

'His room is prepared,' Albert said. 'Waste no more time with him. He will soon hear our demands.'

Simon could not struggle. He felt weak and dizzy. Schengen's grin of hatred made him look more than ever like the goat, and for a few interminable minutes, as Albert forced him forward through a narrow door disguised as a bookcase, Simon almost gave up hope.

He had tried and had failed, but at least Rosina was safe.

The passage down which he stumbled was narrow and cut through the rock. It was well lit and the air was fresh. Only their footsteps broke a menacing silence.

After Albert had opened the next door and pushed Simon forward, he pressed a switch in the passage and his prison was instantly floodlit. All the lighting was from powerful lamps in the high ceiling and corners. Every inch of the rocky chamber was lit. There was no escape from the light, and also high in the walls were four grilles which he was soon to learn covered loud-speakers. There was no furniture except a camp bed and a small steel table riveted to the floor. On the table was a metal jug of water.

'Here you may rest and meditate. We are able to communicate with you and we shall hear anything you have to say. Your decisions will be vital for you, and if satisfactory to us your handcuffs will be removed.'

And that was all. Never before had Simon felt so alone. He sat on the bed and thought of Rosina and her courage as she escaped with Maria. In all the humiliation and confusion of his present situation, he remembered Marston and wondered what had happened to him? He remembered Jake and was encouraged by the thought that, with luck, Rosina and the others would be with him soon.

And it was about then that the whispering began. Softly and seductively at first, in a voice which might have been Schengen's his prison cell was filled with sound. Simon was aware of this type of brainwashing, and although his first reaction of self-defence was to stop his ears, he was curious to know what his enemies wanted from him.

'Relax and rest, Simon. You are again offered an opportunity of changing your life. Such a chance will never come your way again. The publishing venture already discussed is only a part of what can be yours. It is power that is offered to you. Power to change others, to bend them to your will, and so to influence events. Wealth can be yours if you are prepared to throw away some of your outdated ideas, and to join the select few who can lead you along the oldest path of all to a new life … Think about this, Simon … Consider carefully what such power can mean to you and the girl you brought here … There will be times when you can take her anywhere in the world if you use your newfound power over others in the right way …'

This was the sort of temptation offered Simon as he paced up and down in his prison while the harsh lights beat down on him without one shred of friendly shadow.

He knew now that the rumours of the practice of black magic at Les Pins were true. He knew that the power offered to him was dependent upon his acceptance of Satan as lord and master of all, and obeisance would have to be made in front of the worshippers at the mass. And obeisance meant complete renunciation of everything in which he believed. Of everything good, true and beautiful. Of Christianity itself …

And what, Simon wondered, did they want in exchange? What made them think that he would be useful to them? And did they know the truth about Marston and even if they did, what could they do about it? Even if they suspected Peter Pendent? Presumably they were so arrogant that they thought Simon Baines could be bribed to betray them.

The voice was louder now and threatening. 'It is no use sulking, Simon Baines. You have been offered a great opportunity, but if you prefer to stay where you are, you will regret it. You still have time to join us. Nothing in your past life can compare with the power our master offers you … And remember that we shall find your girl and Maria too. We do not like traitors and it is possible for more than one sacrifice to be offered tonight. Consider carefully and remember that we are able to call on the powers of darkness to help your decision.'

Then the lights went out and the sudden silence was as thick as the darkness which enveloped him. Time meant nothing to him now. He raised his hands to his eyes but could not see a finger. Earlier he had been conscious of the muted whine of an air-conditioner, but now that had stopped. All that he could hear was the thudding of his heart.

After a while, he realized that he was in danger of losing control of his will. His mind wandered. He was tempted to give way to the suggestions of betrayal. He forgot that he had been sent to this place for information vital to his country and to the free world. He had no illusions about the strength of the powers of darkness, as he was tempted by his longing for Rosina. Did anything matter as much as their lives together? She deserved the best he could give her. Nothing mattered as much as that. Both of them were too young to be concerned with the sort of moralities which were so important to old squares like Marston. And Peter Pendent in London was only ambitious for himself. Just using others … Anyway what chance was there now for Simon Baines? What was the sense of throwing away the opportunity of a golden future with Rosina?

The darkness pressed on him. The whispering began again. 'We have news for you, Simon. We have your Rosina and the other girl. We shall bring them here for tonight's celebrations. They will both have important parts to play but you can save your girl. When you have told us what we want to know, arrangements can be made for you to go away together … Call us when you are ready.'

And then it was that Simon found his way. It may have been that when he realized the significance of what the whisperer was suggesting, he instinctively remembered and whispered the words hated and feared by all Satanists—*Our Father which art in heaven, Hallowed be Thy name* … And at that moment he knew that his captors were lying. They had already admitted that Rosina had left Vianden and his courage returned. Latour would have sent them on to Jake in Charles's car and it was impossible for *them* to have been followed. Simon was certain that Jake would act on his message that Les Pins should be raided tonight. Rosina would not fail him and neither would he now betray those who had sent him here, nor Marston who had trained him. The hours would be long before he was rescued, but they would pass, so he lifted his fettered hands in the darkness and shouted, 'Are you listening, Schengen? Yes, I'll talk to you when I see Rosina. Bring her to me.'

The moon was hidden by thick clouds as the raiders organized by La Promesse converged on Vianden in three motor coaches with drawn window blinds. The convoy was led by a large car in which travelled Marston, Jake, Jan Schmidt and Rosina. Schmidt and his driver were wearing their regulation 'uniforms' of blue dungarees, Jake a black sweater and Marston his usual shabby tweed suit. Beside him, with her cold hand clasped in his, Rosina prayed that these men would not realize how frightened she was. They stopped for a few minutes outside La Fôret, while Jake went in for a few words with Marguerite Latour. He was smiling grimly when he came back.

'All seems well. The four mechanics we sent ahead arrived safely. Jean is with them now and no doubt the cars of all the visitors to Les Pins have been immobilized … Now Rosina, you will sit next to Jacques and guide him to where the track to Les Pins leaves the road through the forest, and where you say there should be room for the three coaches to park. As soon as the men are out you will lead the four of us to the big gates. If our locksmiths cannot deal with these we have ladders to scale the walls. We shall also force the main door and once we are in you will show us the way to Schengen's room with the goat's head. From the moment you get out of this car Jacques will never leave your side. Jan and I will be near you, but Jacques is your bodyguard and you are to obey him instantly *whatever he says*. He is armed and has his orders, and when you have shown us the room he will take you back to your friends who will be behind our technicians but you will still obey his orders. We shall find your Simon, but we are all relying on you not to make difficulties for us. Will you do as I say? Behind you there will be sixty men pledged to clean up this place and rescue Simon. Don't make it difficult for them by getting in their way or making a scene. Will you obey Jacques whatever happens?'

She wanted to know what Marston would be doing but, as if he could read her thoughts, he released her hand and whispered, 'I shan't be far away. Do as he says.'

So her courage was restored and as she moved into the seat next to Jacques she smiled at Jake and whispered, 'I never thought I would say "Obey" to you, but I will now.'

The wind moaned in the tree-tops of the forest and occasionally a full moon broke through the scudding clouds and touched the turrets and battlements of the château with a silver finger. An owl cried as the forces of evil gathered in the cellars below and the cavalcade of rescuers came slowly up the hill.

Time had no meaning for Simon as the hours passed. His watch had stopped and his captors left him alone. They brought him no food and he was afraid to drink the water which might be drugged. He found some peace in the realization that Rosina must be safe and that help was near. During one period of darkness he slept and woke refreshed until the lights came on again. Occasionally, through tempting thoughts, he felt the pressure of evil, but he knew that his real testing time was still to come, unless his rescuers arrived before the black mass.

They did not, and presently a blurred, almost drunken voice broke the long silence.

'You have not more than an hour to live unless you see reason. Watch the wall now and share with us the honour of homage to our lord and master. Timothy Hitchens is an unworthy sacrifice, but you might save him if you join us. Time is running out for you.'

Then, as the voice stopped and the lights went out, there was a click and what must have been a steel shutter painted to match the rocky walls slid upwards. To his amazement Simon realized that by standing close to what was a small window he could now look down through very thick glass into the old chapel of the château. What he was watching was like television without the sound, but this horrible scene was stark reality.

Instinctively Simon raised his manacled hands and beat on the glass without any effect except his own pain. He was weak and hungry now, and as he realized what was happening a few yards away he almost fainted with shock. The chapel was dimly lit by a few torches on the rocky walls and a row of huge black candles on the ancient altar above which was suspended, *upside down*, a large crucifix. The tortured body of the Christ almost seemed to move in the smoke from the guttering candles.

On the altar itself was stretched the naked body of a man, and with horror Simon realized that the sacrificial victim was Timothy Hitchens. His eyes were closed, his wrists manacled, but he seemed to be breathing. Between the altar and Simon's window the 'worshippers' were crowded. They seemed to be shouting or chanting. All were masked, some were cloaked and a few wore hideous, grotesque animal head-dresses. When the smoke and flames cleared a little he saw, along one wall, tables with the remains of food and drink. One couple was even now sprawled across the débris.

Then, from the shadows behind the altar stepped a scarlet-robed figure with a censer which sent up clouds of smoke. Simon realized that this was a woman and as she leaned across the body on the altar her mask slipped. As she tried to adjust it with one hand he recognized her. She was Timothy's Irish girl-friend Kathie.

As he turned with disgust at such shameful treachery the door of his prison opened. He was too weak to resist the two masked men who each grabbed an arm. One of them had a red beard which Simon had seen before. Neither spoke as they forced him along another passage into the chapel. He choked in the sudden heat and fumes and stumbled, but they held him up and pushed him through the jeering Satanists. A man dressed in a scarlet cassock and wearing a mask of a pig's head, was waiting for him in front of the altar.

'Now what have you to say? Look behind me and see what happens to traitors. Watch carefully but you still have time to save yourself.'

Simon, who suddenly recognized Schengen's voice, held his head high.

'I have nothing to say except that you are a liar, and unless you let me go now to my friends you will regret it.'

Schengen struck him in the face and turned to Red Beard.

'Gag him. Let him see and let him hear. He cannot escape.'

They did that and were not gentle. Simon knew what to expect in a black mass and that it was a parody of the Holy Eucharist. He expected Schengen to be the celebrant, and was amazed when he realized that the enormous man wearing a goat's head mask and a scarlet robe who appeared from the shadows behind the altar must be Albert, and Schengen his server.

Albert first took from the altar and held aloft a gleaming dagger. The worshippers yelled in expectant ecstasy and Simon was reminded of another mob crying 'Crucify Him.' Although he could not understand Albert's words, he knew that he was reciting the Latin mass backwards. Simon also remembered that the climax of the ceremony was the offering to Satan of genuine consecrated wafers from a Christian service which were desecrated in a chalice and then trampled underfoot. This final blasphemy must be approaching and would be the signal for the murder of Timothy.

Simon could bear no more. He struggled to tear the gag from his bleeding mouth, but even if he had been successful nobody would have heard his protest above the yelling of the mob.

As the Great Bear raised the silver chalice in one hand and the dagger in the other, the doors of the chapel burst open. For a few seconds there was silence which was broken by Jake who, with a gun in his hand, shouted to Albert to drop his dagger. And in those seconds Simon, who was only a few steps from the altar, saw Timothy shudder and realized he was still alive. Instinctively he stepped forward and with his fettered hands rolled him off the altar as the weapon came down. Jake's shot shattered Albert's shoulder. The chapel was suddenly full of men in blue dungarees. Women were screaming and cursing as the Satanists were forced into a corner. Kathie tried to defend herself with one of the black candles. Simon, still on his knees saw Schengen struggling to get to him and fumbling under his cassock. And then, miraculously, Marston of all people, also with a gun in his hand, was fighting through the mob to come to him.

'On my way, Simon,' he called and these, typically, were his last words. Kathie struck him on the head with her candle and so he did not see Schengen bring out his own gun. He did not even know who had shot him as he fell forward against Simon.

Four of the men in dungarees disarmed and dealt with Schengen. Another severed Simon's handcuffs and two more carried away the unconscious Timothy. Then Simon saw Rosina pushing Jake aside. She was on her knees beside him and gently took Marston's head on her lap. Her tears fell on his face as Simon tried to find words to comfort her, but all he could say was, 'He saved my life, darling.'

'Of course he did,' she sobbed. 'He was always saving somebody. Always thinking of somebody else. I loved him, Simon, and I always will.'

She loosened the bloodstained shirt and felt for the heart which was no longer beating. She touched a thin, silver chain, lifted it gently and raised the beautiful little crucifix to the other man she loved.

'His best kept secret,' she whispered. 'Something we shall always remember. I'm so proud to have known him.'

'Aren't we all,' Jake said as he helped her gently to her feet. 'And we're proud of you too, my dear. Take her away from this muck-heap, Simon. You've done your job. They've passed this lot over to the police outside and I've got everything we need out of Schengen's safe … Look after him, Rosina.'

She took Simon's arm and helped him as he stumbled through the narrow passages to Schengen's 'Power House' and out of the evil house into the moonlight. Charles and Kate were waiting but tactfully said nothing.

Simon then led her into the shadows and put his arms round her.

'His last words were "On my way, Simon". That's just like him, isn't it? And I've been thinking of his favourite quotation—"The only thing necessary for the triumph of evil, is that good men do nothing." I've had enough, dearest Rosina. Let some other good men do something. All I want is to marry you as soon as possible for ever and a day. I will have to find another job but will you marry me whatever I do?'

'I will,' she whispered. 'For ever and a day.'

This is the last story in this series of Marston Baines Secret Service novels, and the author will be pleased to know what you think of it. You can write to him at his publisher's address:
Malcolm Saville,
c/o William Heineman Ltd,***

*** *We have reproduced the text above from the first edition, but of course it is no longer possible to correspond with Malcolm Saville, who died in 1982. For information about the Malcolm Saville Society, please see page 19.*

GIRLS GONE BY
PUBLISHERS

Girls Gone By Publishers republish some of the most popular children's fiction from the 20th century, concentrating on those titles which are most sought after and difficult to find on the second-hand market. Our aim is to make them available at affordable prices, and to make ownership possible not only for existing collectors but also for new ones, so that the books continue to survive.

As well, we publish some new titles which fit into the genre, including our Chalet School fill-ins, all professionally edited. Authors on the GGBP fiction list include Helen Barber, Elinor Brent-Dyer, Katherine Bruce, Monica Edwards, Amy Fletcher, Antonia Forest, Elizabeth Goudge, Lorna Hill, Phyllis Matthewman, Jane Shaw, Malcolm Saville and Lisa Townsend.

We also publish non-fiction titles, which are lavishly illustrated in black and white.

For details of availability and when to order, see our website or write for a catalogue to GGBP, The Vicarage, Church Street, Coleford, Radstock, Somerset, BA3 5NG, UK.

https://www.ggbp.co.uk/